PRAISE FOR *THE DEAD SPOT: STORIES OF LOST GIRLS*

"A beautifully melancholic collection of stories. These tales of lost girls, of shattered childhoods and broken hearts, of women battling monsters or confronting their darkness, will bury beneath your skin long after the last story has sung its mournful tune. Creative ideas, captivating prose, and aching moments of love, ghosts, art, nightmares, and more, all coalesce into an inventive collection. Sylvaine's storytelling voice is impactful and exciting."

—Sara Tantlinger, Bram Stoker Award-winning author of *The Devil's Dreamland*

"A remarkable collection of stories centered on the themes of obsession, desire, and betrayal that will draw you in with beautiful prose and leave you longing for more from this talented author."

—Christi Nogle, Bram Stoker Award-winning author of *Beulah*

"A beguiling collection of tales that immediately drew me in, chewed me up, and spit me out the other side all the better for it. Angela Sylvaine's debut horror collection is a revelation."

—Caleb Stephens, author of *Feeders* and *The Girls in the Cabin*

"Whether formed in the guise of paper dolls, or forged from the wilderness, the girls in these stories may rise from the depths alone, but they return together, forever changed by the events that shape their stories. Angela Sylvaine strikes with a sharp and stylized wit, claiming her place as a rising star in horror. Filled with sweet surprises and gnawing desires, *The Dead Spot* is a success to be savored."

—Carina Bissett, author of *Dead Girl, Driving & Other Devastations*, and award-winning editor of *Shadow Atlas: Dark Landscapes of the Americas*

THE
DEAD SPOT

STORIES OF LOST GIRLS

CONTENT WARNINGS

Content warnings can be found on page 177.

Reader discretion is advised.

Edited by Rob Carroll
Book Design and Layout by Rob Carroll

ISBN 978-1-958598-27-6 (paperback)
ISBN 978-1-958598-62-7 (eBook)

darkmatter-ink.com

THE
DEAD SPOT

STORIES OF LOST GIRLS

ANGELA SYLVAINE

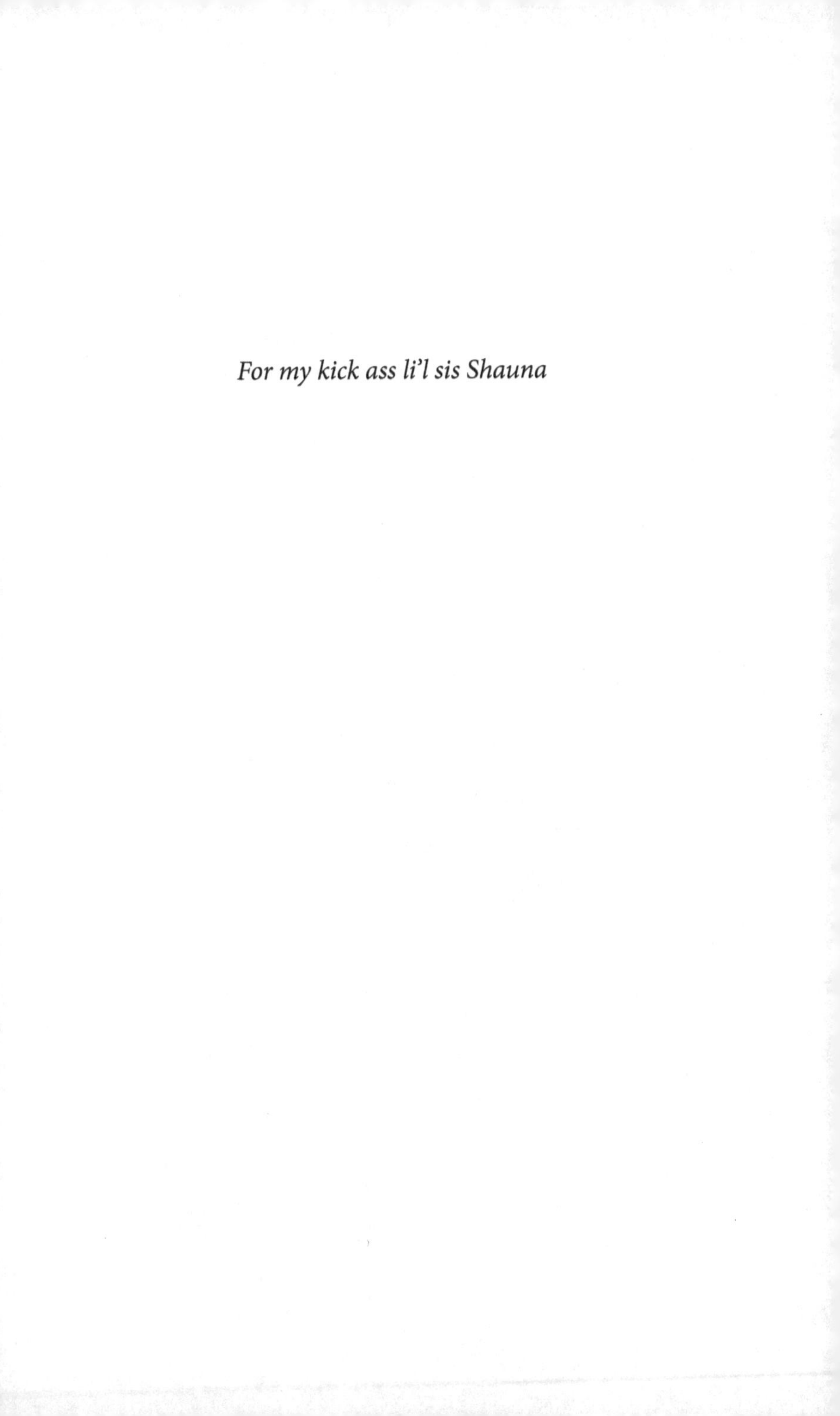

For my kick ass li'l sis Shauna

CONTENTS

FOREWORD

DON'T LET THE Cheerful Goth fool you—Angela Sylvaine is vicious.

I first met Angela on Twitter, where she's been a supportive and vital member of the horror community. She's a champion for her fellow writers, cheering wins, promoting projects, and sharing her skills and knowledge to help others succeed. Her infectious smile brightens your screen, whether it's in a social media post or The Cheerful Goth Newsletter. She's wicked and funny. It's a gift to know her, to be her friend.

Then you read her work.

Angela's short fiction remains grounded in a humanness, a clear empathy towards her characters, no matter how fantastical or familiar the setting may be. This lulls you into the comfort and security of identifying with her characters, rooting for them, believing that they will not only survive but triumph because they have to, because so many of them are good people (whether it's on the surface, deep down, or fully-formed in the vulnerability of their flaws and questionable motivations). We believe their perceptions and intentions—we believe in *them*—as they make choices we can see ourselves making. They have to win.

Then you read a story like "Playing Tricks."

Vicious. So vicious that, after reading, I put the book down and said, "Damn, what else is she hiding in that brain?"

Don't worry, though. I can assure you that though Angela Sylvaine may be observing us, adding to her extensive knowledge of how people interact and destroy each other, she's keeping the blade in her bag. For now.

I recently had the pleasure of speaking on a panel at StokerCon 2023 in Pittsburgh with Angela. She assured me she was nervous, too, but the way she commanded the room with her humor, wit, and confidence—you never would've known. She had the audience laughing and engaged, and all of the panelists eager to keep the conversation going.

All of that wit, a little of that humor, and a heaping dose of deadly charm is evident in Angela's work. I don't know if she would agree, but I see a lot of Angela as a person in her stories. That wit comes out in that ever-vicious (and one of my favorites) "Playing Tricks," where she not only turns a well-worn trope on its head but gives us an ending that manages to surprise, satisfy, and enrage all at once. There's more of that wit and plenty of razor-blade-studded charm in "Antifreeze and Sweet Peas," where good intentions get knotted up in cinematic twists and turns. A shot of bitter humor lightly tinges the strange and heartbreaking logic of children in "Mr. Chew." Angela's confidence shines through in another of my favorites, "Starved," where the characters are fully formed in all their flaws and desires, their every action charged with need and ache.

There's all the delicious chills and thrills, and plenty of wicked fun in Angela Sylvaine's work, but make no mistake, she will also make you cry. You'll bleed empathy for Ellie in "Astronaut Dreams." You'll ache with recognition for Farrah in the inventive and lyrical "Burnt Embers and Bluebirds." If you've ever lost a love of any kind, "Sorry, We're Open" will break you.

Rest assured, though. Despite the desperation and pain of these characters, you won't finish this collection heartbroken. There is more here than what you see. Angela digs deeper, reflecting our current and often dismal reality, like in the dark tale of urban gentrification "Clutching Air." She shines a light on the neglected and invisible in "Edge of Decay." Like in real life, her protagonists often fight a losing battle, and we mourn for them, unable to look away, in their struggles that are all too familiar. But sometimes, we get the gleeful satisfaction of vengeance. Every one of her characters fights hard, making their wins all the sweeter and their losses all the more heartrending.

The stories in *The Dead Spot: Stories of Lost Girls* focus on a variety of women and girls in terrible situations, whether they are victims of something outside their control, or in a turmoil of their own making. Each character Angela Sylvaine creates is distinct, with a fully drawn point of view—a down-and-out bride obsessed with a wedding dress that may change her life, a teen yearning for freedom in her tightly structured existence, a little girl utilizing her imagination to survive some sort of apocalypse. All these women and girls have several things in common: they are often lonely, misunderstood, and desperate for a connection they can't quite reach. And in that struggle for connection, they sometimes end up destroying the very thing they want most.

But maybe the most important thing the characters of *The Dead Spot* have in common: they have agency. Victim or aggressor, no matter how others view them, these characters will not be silent. They won't accept their fate. They will fight.

These two through lines not only strengthen but breathe life into the stories in these pages. Angela Sylvaine doesn't just create tragic girls or monstrous women, leaving them to suffer through futile battles for our entertainment. She fights for her characters. She is their creator and their advocate. You'll cheer for every one of these women and girls, even as they descend into darkness.

And that brings me back to the duality of Angela Sylvaine as The Cheerful Goth. How can someone make you laugh and break your heart at the same time? How can a smile that bright be so deadly? Nothing is ever simple in the stories of *The Dead Spot*. You'll read this collection with the lights on, glancing behind you at every noise, every shadow, every moment of looming dread. You might even see yourself in these pages.

Don't let Angela Sylvaine fool you. Her blade is sharp, but her pen is even deadlier.

—J. A. W. McCarthy
September 2023

ASTRONAUT DREAMS

DAY 1

ELLIE LOPED ACROSS the dirt road after her big sister, barreling into the field of giant sunflowers. Her white, army-surplus hazmat suit was bunched at the wrists and ankles, where they met her gloved hands and bootied feet, too big for her pre-teen body. Sweat matted her chin-length curls to her head beneath the clear plastic mask and hood.

Barb stopped beneath the Oak tree that towered over the flowers, flipping her blonde ponytail over one shoulder. "Will you take that ridiculous thing off?"

"Can't. I'm in astronaut training." The suit had been a birthday gift from her dad and was her most prized possession. She'd used silver duct tape to ring the knees, elbows, and waist, and to attach an American flag patch to the chest.

Ellie had her whole life planned out. She'd enlist in the Air Force like her dad, become a hero pilot, get promoted to officer, and become an astronaut for NASA. Maybe her mom would even see Ellie on the news and come back, realize she'd been wrong to leave them.

"You're so weird." Barb dampened the remark with an affectionate grin.

A prop plane buzzed overhead, misting the field with whatever chemical concoction they used to make the sunflowers grow so big.

Ellie waved her free hand over her head, the other occupied with a pair of hedge clippers. "Hellllloooo up there." She dreamed of the plane someday skidding to a stop on the road and offering to take her for a spin.

"Better not let Dad see you," Barb said. "He's convinced Cultivar is the reason the crops are so sparse this year."

Ellie glanced across the road toward their farm—a two-story house needing a coat of paint, a barn that looked ready to fall over, two cylindrical silos, and a field of sugar beets whose green tops were half the size of a normal year.

"But that doesn't make sense. Cultivar makes things grow bigger." She reached out a white gloved hand to grip the thick stalk of the sunflower beside her. The thing came up to her shoulder, and its head was as big as her own.

"Not always. Haven't you ever heard of Monsanto?"

A honeybee landed on the sunflower, flitting among the tiny brown florets in the center. "Mon-what?"

"Never mind. Give me the clippers." Barb held out one hand, distractedly watching the cluster of trees beside the house. Their dad had ventured into the woods to hunt pheasant, hoping to bag a few birds for dinner, but it was impossible to know how long he'd be gone. He may not like Cultivar, but he didn't approve of them snipping flowers, either.

Ellie began to raise the sheers, handing them to her sister sharp-end first, then stopped, frowning. More bees had joined the one on the flower, but they were fighting rather than feeding. There were at least a dozen, buzzing and barreling into each other. She surveyed the field and saw more of them appear every second, until the insects were so thick in the air above the flowers that they resembled a writhing storm cloud.

"Ow, get off!" Barb yelled, drawing Ellie's attention back to her.

Ellie froze.

Bees surrounded Barb's head, her hair and face teeming with the buzzing insects. She swatted at them, but they only grew more aggressive. Red welts bloomed on the skin of her face and arms.

"Dad, help!" Ellie screamed, her panicked breath steaming her plastic face mask.

Barb snapped her gaze to Ellie and stood rigidly straight. The bees rose, joining the cloud overhead.

"Are you okay?" Ellie asked. "What do I do?"

The whites of Barb's eyes pooled with blood, and her lips drew back to bare her straight white teeth. She lunged, arms outstretched and fingers curled into claws.

Ellie raised her hands to block her sister's attack, but she still clutched the clippers with the pointed end angled out and up. Barb barreled into Ellie, and as they fell through the thick stalks of the sunflowers, the weight of Barb's body drove the sharpened twin blades of the clippers through the soft patch of skin under her chin, embedding the tool all the way up to the handles. The thicket of flowers enclosed them in shadow.

Ellie shrieked and rolled Barb off her. She knelt by her big sister, whose mouth gaped like a dying fish. She gripped the handles of the clippers and pulled, releasing a spray of blood that stained her gloved hands red.

Barb coughed once, splattering Ellie's mask, then went limp. Her head thumped to the ground, eyes wide and slack mouth leaking blood.

Ellie scrambled backward, trembling. "It was an accident. I didn't mean to. Barb?" Sobs caught in her chest. She clawed at the hood and mask, needing to breathe, needing fresh air, but her grip was too slippery. "Barb, wake up. I'm sorry, just wake up!"

Wide, dead eyes stared back from her big sister's face.

Dad would know what to do, he would help her. She got up and ran, the sunflowers smacking against her arms, her shoulders, her head. "Dad! Help!" she screamed, racing across the dirt road.

He stepped from the woods beside the house, holding a shotgun pointed at the ground and peering at her from beneath the brim of his dirty work cap. His mouth twisted in a frown, and he jogged toward her.

Buzzing enveloped her, surrounding her and echoing through her ears. She closed her eyes and clapped her hands over her ears, dropping to the ground of the front yard. She waited for the sharp stings, but they never came. The buzzing dimmed, releasing her, and she looked up, her heart thundering in her chest.

The bees encased her dad, seemed to consume him.

"Dad!"

"Stop!" he yelled, holding out a hand covered with squirming bees.

She froze, just like she had with Barb.

A guttural scream ripped from his throat.

She forced herself to stand, stumbling as her bootied feet slipped on the grass. She hadn't been able to help Barb, but it wasn't too late for her dad. "Hold on!" she yelled, snagging the hose that lay coiled in the grass.

She raised the sprayer, her hand slipping on the trigger, and met his gaze. His eyes had turned crimson. With a grunt, he wedged the shotgun beneath his chin and pulled the trigger.

Ellie jolted as if electrocuted and collapsed to her knees.

DAY 473

ELLIE TORE OFF a strip of duct tape with her teeth and slapped it over the small tear that had appeared on the upper arm of her white, army-surplus suit. She'd torn off the American flag patch that had decorated the chest, knowing she wasn't worthy, would never be a hero. When her sister and dad were attacked, Ellie hadn't saved them.

After adjusting her plastic face mask beneath the hood and slipping her booties over her sandaled feet, she shuffled down the steps of the old farmhouse. The field to the side of the house was dead, filled with shriveled and yellowing remnants of beet plants. With no gasoline to power the machinery needed to water and harvest the crops, she'd had to let them die.

Out of habit, she scanned left and right before crossing the dirt road, though the only vehicles that passed now were military trucks. The field that had once bloomed with giant sunflowers had been clear-cut, giant threshers pulverizing the plants into compost. Initially, they thought destroying the food source of the bees would stop the epidemic, but those bees didn't want flowers, they wanted blood.

Ellie walked across uneven soil peppered with rocks and the sprouts of Kentucky bluegrass, and toward a gnarled oak tree. Beneath the tree, two wood crosses had been stuck into the ground. Those first days alone, she'd concentrated all her energy, all her guilt and sadness, on digging the holes, constructing the crosses, and dragging the bodies of her dad and big sister to their resting places, all while encased in her protective suit.

Blackberry vines trailed across the dirt and crept up the tree's trunk. She'd found the fruit seeds in the pantry and sprinkled them around the graves. The bushes now bloomed with lush, sweet berries, and they had attracted ants, who traipsed though the sparse grass to claim fallen fruit and haul it back to the burrows that rose from the dirt in tiny mounds. The ants reminded her that life was resilient, and that you had to work hard to survive. They gave her a little hope.

She looked at the smaller of the two graves. "Hi, Barb. Have you forgiven me yet?" It didn't matter to Ellie that Barb had gone mad out there in the sunflowers that day. In her mind, she was the one who killed her. "Yeah, me neither."

Every day she wished she'd been the one to get bit, that Barb had been the one with astronaut dreams.

"Morning, Dad." She hadn't killed her dad; he'd done that to himself. She couldn't know for sure, but she thought he felt the change coming on, felt the overwhelming rage, and he'd killed himself to stop from hurting her.

Besides the ants, those two lumps of earth were her only company. In the early days, she at least had the TV, could watch the news reports. Cultivar had sprayed fields across the country with their miracle fertilizer, changing the genetics of the plants. They weren't harmful to humans or most animals, even when eaten, but that wasn't the case for bees. The pollen acted like a powerful steroid, turning docile honeybees into blood-thirsty zombees. When the zombees stung, their venom transformed the victim within a matter of seconds, even with a single sting.

It took several days after the first attacks for the scientists to understand what was happening, and by then hundreds of thousands of people were dead or infected. Some didn't believe in the epidemic, called it hoax, and walked right out into the swarms of zombees. The first time Ellie had seen that footage, she'd screamed at the TV, begged the people to stop.

By the end of the first week, the government had sent troops to every corner of the country to kill the infected plants. Citizens were warned to isolate in their homes and never go outside with exposed skin, told that the zombees would die off eventually. But the bees were merely the first stage of the epidemic, and things only got worse. Food shortages, failure of the electrical grids, and rioting followed.

Lucky for Ellie, she lived in a rural area, had a well-stocked pantry, and was able to keep up with any news through her solar-powered AM radio. At first, she tried waving down the military trucks, but they never stopped, didn't care about one random little girl. After the first month alone, she walked to town, hoping to discover survivors, but she'd found only zombees and one of them almost caught her.

That had been more than a year ago now, and she couldn't stay sheltered in her house any longer. Her pantry supplies had dwindled to almost nothing. She had already packed up the last of the food and planned her hike down the road, in the direction of the military trucks. They'd be forced to take her in if she showed up at the base, and maybe they could even help her find her mother, if she was still alive.

"I miss you both so much." Her throat tight, Ellie turned away from the graves of her dad and big sister.

She stepped gingerly over the spreading blackberry vines, and her foot sunk into a soft patch of soil. Something beneath the dirt poked her foot, tearing the fabric of her suit. "Shit." She bent down to inspect the tear that revealed her sandal-clad foot. There weren't any bees around that she could see, but she'd need to tape the hole to be safe.

Crouching, she trailed her gloved hand through the soil in search of whatever had poked her foot. A bit of metal presented itself, and she pushed the dirt away to reveal the sharp end of the hedge clippers now stained with blood. She cringed and backed away, her mind flashing to the memory of Barb's face, the clippers speared through her chin.

The blackberry vines caught on Ellie's ankle, and she stumbled, stepping on a teaming anthill with her partially exposed foot.

"Ow!" she cried, as a sharp pain stung her big toe. She yanked back her foot and looked down to see a single bee wiggling its way out of the anthill.

She sucked in a breath and held it, shaking so hard she might crack to pieces. A wave of searing rage roared up her body and crashed through her head in a wave that destroyed all thought.

Tearing off her hood and mask, Ellie howled the scream of a monster as her vision turned blood red.

THE BRIDE

SOMETHING CATCHES MY hand, pulls me back toward the stall. I shriek, assaulted by images of tiny, porcelain hands clawing at me. My cheeks heat at the sight of my engagement ring caught on a piece of fabric.

I've been meaning to get the bent prong repaired, but the store clerk will give me that look. Eli promised he'll get me a real diamond someday. I unhook myself from the delicate lace and freeze as I register the single article of clothing hung beside the black-eyed dolls with their matted hair.

A dress. My dress.

I close my eyes and imagine myself as a bride, my auburn hair piled on my head, curls spilling down my neck and tumbling over my shoulders. The Victorian-style gown of delicate golden lace and fine beading shimmers under the lights. The boned corset nips in at the waist, giving way to a full skirt that bursts over my hips and flows to the floor.

The vision fades, and I sag against the wall, gasping for breath. The sweet taste of cake and the pleasant sting of champagne bubbles linger on my tongue.

"Rose, you're losing it," I say to no one in particular. I've finally cracked. My pre-wedding jitters are mutating into full-blown psychosis.

I lift the dress from its hook to check under each arm and inside the neckline for a price tag. My wallet holds fifty bucks cash and my bank account a measly two hundred, even with all the extra shifts I've been picking up at the restaurant. I clutch the dress to my chest and rush toward the front of the store.

A stick of an old man in a flannel shirt, unnecessary suspenders attached to his polyester pants, sits behind the counter. He runs a finger down the page of a ledger book, a pair of spectacles perched on his nose.

"Hello, sir? This doesn't have a price tag." I cringe at the frantic wobble in my voice.

He grunts and reaches toward me. I release my hold on the gown, letting him pull it across the counter. His hand shakes with tremors as he sweeps the dress for a tag.

"I already checked." I rub my damp hands down the front of my jeans.

"Where'd ya get it?" he asks.

"Sorry?" Has the old guy gone senile and forgotten this is a store?

He glares at me over his glasses with eyes milky from cataracts. "Which stall?"

"Oh, right." I point toward the back of the store. "The one with the dolls."

"Widow Montgomery never was able to have kids of her own." He tugs the ledger out from under the dress to flip through the pages. The binding of the book creaks with each movement, and the musty smell of old paper tickles my nose. "Collected those damn dolls until they took her off to the home."

I reach out, ready to yank the book from his hands and find the darn page myself, but I stop myself. What in world has come over me? I paste on a smile.

He stops flipping and runs his finger down the page. "Nothin' here." His lips pull down at the corners, taking the rest of his face with them.

"Maybe it got moved from another stall." I stand on my toes, craning my neck to see the ledger. "Could you please look in the other ones, sir?"

"I don't remember no dress, and I know this place inside and out." He slams the book closed, releasing a puff of dust into the air.

"Well, what would you want for it?" I swallow past the dryness in my mouth and throat. "I don't have much money, but I could make payments." Please, God, let me have this dress. I'll do anything, pay any price.

"The folks who rent the stalls set the prices. Can't sell it without knowing where it came from." He begins to pull the rest of the gown over the counter.

"No, please." I grab onto the skirt, curling my fingers in the layers of lace and taffeta. My eyes blur with tears.

He sneers and points one bony finger in my face. "Are you deaf, or just stupid? Can't sell it without a price." He mumbles under his breath. "Bitch needs to learn some respect."

His words cut me like a switch against bare skin. I shove down my pride and ready myself to beg and plead, to promise anything if only he'll give me the dress.

I open my mouth to speak when the lights in the store flicker. A second later, the bare bulb hanging behind the counter shatters with a pop, sending a sprinkling of glass shards through the air to land in the old man's thinning gray hair. He cries out and swipes his hand across the back of his neck.

His fingertips come away smeared with blood.

I tug the dress out of his reach, cradle the gown in my arms. I stroke my fingers across the bodice. I must protect it.

The old man glares at me.

"Are you hurt, sir?"

He pulls a rag from his pocket, wiping his fingers and neck. "Just a scratch, is all." He reaches out for the gown. "Give it here."

I shrink back and tighten my hold on the dress as the lights give another flicker and go out. A chill settles over me, and I suppress a shudder.

Sunlight streams through the glass front door of the shop, illuminating the area near the counter, but darkness blankets the rear of the store. I take a step in that direction. "Hello? Is anyone back here?" The thought of being stuck alone in the pitch-black with those creepy dolls sends a shiver up my spine.

The old man gasps. "Goddamn pacemaker." He slips from his stool and clutches his chest with one hand. He grasps the countertop with the other. "Don't just stand there, gawkin'. Call 9-1-1."

"Okay. You're going to be okay." I fish my phone from my pocket one-handed and punch in the digits with my thumb. Stay calm, Rose, stay calm. "Help will be here soon."

He hunches forward and thumps his fist against his chest. "Goddamn VA piece of garbage."

I still cradle the dress in the crook of my left arm, and I swear it twists in my grip. My finger freezes above the send button. "So, how much did you say for the dress?"

The lights flip back on, bathing the store in light.

I LAY THE dress, wrapped in a clear plastic bag, down inside the trunk of my beat-up Honda Accord and close the lid. My entire body is numb as I walk around the car, open the door, and climb into the driver's seat.

Red and blue lights flash atop the ambulance parked near the front of the store. The paramedics wheel the old man out on a gurney and slide him into the back of the vehicle, an oxygen mask covering his face.

I grip the steering wheel, hot from the sun, and try to stop my hands from shaking. My stomach churns, sending bile into my throat. I gag but manage to swallow it back down.

What the heck is wrong with me?

That man could have died all because I had to have the dress. I rest my forehead on the wheel, and I cry. Not a little sniffle, but a shoulder-shaking, snot-dripping cry.

PARKED IN A space at the front of the lot beside my apartment building, I pop open my trunk. My heart skips at the sight of the dress. It's really mine. A flicker of guilt nags me at how I manipulated the old man, but I push it away. He still got help, and I got my dress.

From behind me, arms wind around my waist, and I yelp.

"Relax Rosie-Posie, it's just me." Eli nuzzles my neck.

I giggle and spin around, slinging my arms around his neck. "You know I hate that nickname." He gave it to me in foster care, after the nursery rhyme "Ring Around the Rosie," and the darn thing stuck.

"Liar. You like it." He grins, his brown eyes twinkling with laughter. His blond hair is a little long and flops into his eyes.

I try for a scowl but can't pull it off. "What are you doing here?"

"Decided to use my lunch break to come see my girl." He strokes his thumb across my cheek.

I push up on my tiptoes and plant a kiss on his lips. "Smooth talker."

"What's that?" He angles his head to peak over my shoulder.

I smile so big my face aches. "I found a dress."

"It's a miracle." He wraps me in a hug and spins me in a circle.

I laugh and scream. "Put me down."

He releases me and reaches into the trunk.

"No." I back up, blocking him with my body. He's going to try and take the dress, but I can't let him. I have to protect it.

Eli crosses his arms. "Come on. I only want a peak."

A nervous giggle escapes my throat. Of course, he wouldn't take the dress. That's ridiculous. "No peaking until the big day, you know that." I lightly smack his chest. "Now get out of here. I still need to try it on."

"Alright." He places a kiss on the tip of my nose. "Love you, Rosie-Posie."

"Love you, too." I blow him a kiss.

Sitting on my bumper, I watch him walk away. I still can't believe we're getting married. He's been the only good thing in my life for so long, and I get to keep him forever. I barely manage to suppress a squeal of joy, wrapping my arms around myself to hold it in.

Shaking my head, I return my attention to the dress and scoop it from the trunk.

My apartment is on the top floor of a rundown brick building which used to be a motel. There is no elevator, just outdoor concrete stairs that connect each floor.

Tucker, the little terrier belonging to Mrs. Patterson in 2D is tied to the railing at the bottom of the steps.

"Hey, little guy." I stoop to pet him.

His muzzle wrinkles and he lunges forward, snapping his teeth and growling.

I gasp and stumble backward.

He growls and barks in my direction, tugging on his leash until I think it might snap.

"What's wrong with you, grumpy?" I frown and tromp up the stairs, while Tucker barks away in the background. My arms ache from the weight of the gown, but I make it up the four flights to my floor, sweat dripping down my back.

I manage to fumble my keys from my purse and open the door. The heat trapped inside hits me like in a wave, and I flip on the ceiling fan before closing the door. Tenants are expected to furnish their own AC, but I can't afford it.

My convertible sofa bed sits against the far wall of the single room apartment, and I lay the dress across the faded blue cushions. I cross back to the single window, next to the door, and tug the curtains closed to block out the sun. A small table next to the sofa holds a lamp, and I flip it on.

I kneel before the dress and remove the protective garbage bag. Somehow, it's even more beautiful than I remember. Part of me panics a little. What if it doesn't fit? I undress, discarding my hideous orange waitress uniform and apron in a pile on the floor. Parting the heavy, layered skirt, I slip the dress over my head. The length is just right, the hem barely skimming the floor. The back lacing is tricky, but I manage to reach behind me and tug the ribbons tight.

The dress fits perfectly, as if custom made just for me. The bodice hugs my body, accentuating my chest and narrowing my waist, and the intricate beading along the top is beautiful, with just a few spots needing repairs.

A grin splits my face as I spin in the center of the room, the full skirt billowing like a blooming flower. My bare feet dance across the carpeted floor, and warmth fills my entire body. I will be the most beautiful bride anyone has ever seen.

This dress is going to be the perfect start to the rest of my life.

SOMETHING WRENCHES ME awake.

"Hello, is anyone there?" I sit upright in my fold-out bed, clutching the sheet to my chest. My heart thumps and fear hums through my veins.

I feel eyes on me. I'm not alone.

A shaft of light from the streetlamp pierces the darkness through a crack in the curtains. The front door is closed, and my cramped kitchenette is empty and quiet. The bathroom door to my left sits wide open, giving full view of the small space. Empty.

My breath catches at the sight of my closet. The accordion-style doors are wide open, though I remember closing them. My dress lies in a heap on the floor, its hanger still swaying on the bar.

"Is anyone here?"

There must be someone here, hiding. I lean over the side of the bed, my hair brushing the floor as I peer into the shadows. Nothing, and there is nowhere else to go.

Someone tried to break in and steal my dress.

They must have run away. Probably that old man from the antique store, deciding he wanted to keep the gown for himself just to spite me. Bastard.

I glance at the front door again. It's locked with a chain, and no one could have disengaged that lock from the outside. Be reasonable, Rose. The old man is sick. He has more important things to think about than some dress. Besides, I paid in cash, so he doesn't even know my name.

These wedding jitters are really starting to mess with my brain.

Pushing away my bedding, I shuffle to my closet and lift the dress by the shoulders to hold it aloft. A coldness passes over me, through me, chilling to the bone even in the summer heat. The draft follows me as I lay the dress out on one side of the bed, on top of the covers. Better to have the gown close, so I can make sure it's safe. I climb into bed on the other side, shivering from the cold, and pull the covers over me. I rest one hand on the bodice of the dress. If anyone tries to take it from me, I'll be ready.

A BUZZING SOUND coaxes me from a deep sleep. I try desperately to grasp the last vestiges of my dream. A blond woman spins around and around before a mirror in my dress, her face glowing with happiness. The image flits through my mind and is gone.

I reach over and touch the satin and beading of the gown. Still here, still safe.

Buzz, buzz, buzz.

I feel around the bedside table until I find my phone, which shows a missed call and a voicemail from my best friend, Dinah. I hit play.

"Rose, where are you? We're already a person short with Manny quitting. Get your ass in here," she says.

"Crap." I must have slept through my alarm or forgotten to set one. Morning sunlight streams through the crack in the curtains. Breakfast is the busiest time at the restaurant, and Dinah must be going crazy trying to handle it all herself. I should jump out of bed and get down there as fast as possible. Lord knows I need the money.

My heartbeat flutters in my chest, a quick, staccato beat. I can't leave, not now. I survey my apartment. Someone was here last night. What if they try to break in again? I pull the dress across the bed and settle it on my lap.

I text a quick reply to Dinah. *Sick as a dog, so can't come in. Sorry:(*

Guilt churns through my stomach, and I grimace. I've never lied to her, but I have no choice. I must protect the dress.

The cold is back. It lays on top of me like a lead weight, sinking onto my chest, through my ribs, into my heart. Goosebumps break out across my arms, and the hair on the back of my neck stands up.

I clutch the dress tighter, using it as a blanket, but the chill seems to get worse.

IT'S TAKEN ME all day, but I've managed to mend every loose bead, every unraveling hem, every torn bit of lace. My fingertips are bloody and sore from the needle, and I make sure to wrap them with bandages so no blood stains the delicate fabric of the dress.

It's perfect, just as it was so many years ago.

My eyelids drift closed as the lilting melody of a waltz plays through my mind. The fair-haired bride is back, spinning and laughing. She's thinking about her fiancée, about the look on his face when he sees her on their special day.

The music and laughter fade as the image transforms. Now the woman sits on a chaise lounge wearing an old-fashioned cotton nightgown. Silent sobs wrack her body, and she rocks in place. She clutches the dress to her chest, knowing she'll never get that chance to wear it. Why did her father have to be so cruel and send her dearest Brock away?

Don't cry, Anna. Don't cry.

A pounding noise wrenches me back to reality, and I blink back the tears brimming in my eyes.

"Rosie, it's me." Eli's voice carries through the door.

The dress. He can't be allowed to see it. I glance at the closet, at the empty hanger on the bar. The closet isn't safe. I need to be able to see the gown, touch it.

A faint electrical buzzing sounds beside me, and the lamp flickers off. I tap the bulb with my finger.

Thump, thump, thump.

"You're freaking me out, baby. Open up so I can see you're okay." His voice is tight, tense.

I creep across the apartment. Leaving the chain fastened, I open the door a crack and peek through.

"Dinah said you called in sick."

I cringe at the worry in his voice. "I caught some kind of bug." The lie leaves a sour taste on my tongue.

"You should have called me." He lifts the plastic grocery bag in his hand. "Anyway, I brought soup and cold medicine."

I smile. Maybe I can put the gown away and let him in for a few minutes.

A buzz sounds behind me, and I glance over my shoulder. The lamp flickers on, seeming to get brighter, then goes off with a pop. The dress on the bed ripples slightly, as if brushed by a breeze.

I peer up at Eli. "I don't want to get you sick."

"I'll be fine." He pushes against the door. "Come on, let me in."

"No." I clutch the door jam, sending a sting of pain through my battered fingers. "I just need to get some rest."

He backs up a step. "Oh…okay. I guess I'll just leave this for you." He puts the bag down. "Call me tomorrow?"

I flinch at the uncertainty in his voice. "I will. Promise."

"Love you, Rosie." He stands there, staring at me, his shoulders slumped.

My throat tightens. "Love you, too." I close the door and lean against it. Part of me wants to fling open the door and rush after him, do anything to wipe that look of hurt from his face, but I can't leave. Not now. Once I'm sure the dress is safe, protected, I'll make it up to him.

I DON'T NORMALLY wear much makeup, but this is a special occasion. Eyeliner, shadow, mascara, and lipstick. I even take extra time to curl my auburn mane before piling it on my head. Finally, I'm ready. As I slip on the gown and lace up the back, tension melts from my muscles.

The sensation of being watched sends a quiver along my spine, and I scan the room, my eyes darting into every corner, peering into every shadow.

I'm all alone.

I should take off the dress, I know, but the thought of removing the gown makes my heart pound so hard it echoes through my bones. I'll just wear it for a little while longer. I sway and turn in the center of the room, dancing to the music lilting through my mind.

The shard of sunlight that streams through the curtains dims then disappears, replaced by the light of the streetlamp as day turns to night. I've been dancing so long my feet ache and throb.

I should rest a minute. The dress will be fine as long as I'm careful. I lie back on my bed, on top of the covers.

I drift in and out of sleep, for how long I'm not sure.

The shard of sunlight is back.

My phone buzzes on the nightstand.

Someone pounds on the door, shouting my name.

I barely register the disturbance.

The coldness is with me again. I turn my head and see the bride lying beside me on the bed. She is the most beautiful woman I have ever seen. Pale, alabaster skin. Blue eyes that sparkle like sapphires. Lips red as ripe strawberries. Golden hair fanned across the pillow.

"Anna," I whisper. I want to reach out, but I'm afraid my touch will send her away.

She places her hand on my cheek. Her caress is ice, biting my skin, and the frost spreads through my body.

I want to pry her hand away, but I can't move.

I can't move.

Fear sends my heart galloping in my chest. I breathe faster and faster. Every inch of my skin is numb with cold.

She smiles, and her skin cracks like old porcelain. Black sludge wells in the cracks, oozing out in thick drops. Her golden hair turns gray and begins to fall from her scalp in clumps as her eyes melt in a stream of yellowy puss that runs down her face. The red of her lips turns flaky and brown, like drying blood, and her teeth rot and crumble.

I try to scream but only manage a faint moan. Every inch of my body, inside and out, is frozen. My pulse slows as the blood in my veins turns to slush. Each breath a struggle, I gasp for air as arctic flames engulf my skin. A silent scream fills my throat.

My vision begins to blur at the edges. Hold on. Stay awake.

A faint pounding reaches my ears. The door. I can't even open my mouth to cry out.

I love you, Eli.

A single teardrop freezes in the corner of my eye.

Anna wraps her arms around me and pulls me close. I try to thrash, to break free, but my body is no longer mine to control. I want to scream and beg, but my lungs are locked in ice. The rotten odor of death surrounds me.

The Daily Mirror

LOCAL BRIDE FREEZES TO DEATH IN HOME

POLICE ARE SEARCHING for answers in the death of 21-year-old Rose Halloway, whose body was found in her apartment early yesterday morning. Police discovered the body after her fiancé reported hearing a struggle inside. Clothed in her wedding dress, Halloway was unconscious and not breathing when found. Attempts to revive her failed. The apparent cause of death is hypothermia, which has officials baffled. Investigators are calling the death of Halloway suspicious. Anyone with information should contact the police department.

NEW HUE

TOX TRIED COTTON candy once, back when she wiggled through a gap in the wall during Spree. She had been hiding in the shadows, watching the beautiful people pass in their fine clothes, carrying stuffed peacocks or panthers, when a boy threw away a paper cone still sticky with the sugary remnants, and Tox fished it from the garbage. The sweetness singed her taste buds in a way that made the beating from the Sentry worth every bruise.

She had that same feeling when she saw the Matriarch. Their ruler visited Lowtown to ensure the diggers, the cutters, the scavengers, and the rest, kept up their work. The sight of the Matriarch, a rare Pink, melted into Tox's eyes like candy. Lips of crushed flower petals, shattered rose-quartz eyes, and hair to match the most glorious pink sunset. The scent of toasted marshmallows wafted through the air, rolling from the Matriarch in waves.

Lying on the dirt floor of her shack, chisel clutched for protection, Tox dreamt of being a Chroma. But she'd been born a Stone, a Lesser, thought she would never shine like a Pink, Thought she'd always blend in with the chunks of rock she honed and carved for use in the skyscrapers. Until she found a torn and trampled section of a newspaper with an ad on the back.

NEW HUE

=

NEW YOU

☆ Revel in Every Color on the Spectrum

☆ Apricot, Crimson, Amethyst, Jade,

Caramel, and More

☆ For a Limited Time: Dianthus Pink

☆ Priced from 150 to 700 Credits

☆ Full Transformation Guaranteed

☆ Available at New Hue Automats

*EFFECTS LAST TWENTY-FOUR HOURS

DIANTHUS PINK. THE rarest of Chroma. The color of cotton candy and the Matriarch.

Tox had just over seven hundred credits stored on the card buried in her dirt floor. Credits she planned to spend on a pod in upper Lowtown when one opened, enough to pay rent for a full year. Throat tight, she let the clipping slip from her fingers to land in the muddy puddle at her feet.

Something struck her forehead, and she winced, pressing her fingers to the wound. They came away tinged gray. Beside her, an old man, a Rust, cried out and fell to his knees.

Laughter erupted from the wall, where several Chroma kids sat, pellet guns raised.

"Told ya. They even bleed filthy," one said.

Tox helped the man to his feet and led him to shelter. He lived just down from her, had known her mother when she was still alive, before the dust and grit filled her lungs so she could no longer breathe.

"You okay?" Tox asked, earning only a grunt. His skin hung off his skull, and she figured he'd soon be dead, too. She saw herself reflected in his vacant eyes, knew that she'd end up like him soon enough.

TOX WORKED NIGHTS chiseling a hole in the wall large enough for her thin frame. She slipped through, something she hadn't done in years. The streets near the wall were quiet, though sounds of music and raucous voices carried from the center of the city.

She crept along the buildings, wondering which of the bricks had been carved by her hands, by her mother's. The road shone in the light of the streetlamps whose metalwork was crafted by Rusts like the old man who'd been shot.

A row of Automats lined the sidewalk, selling food, clothing, and all manner of devices powered by Lesser-mined zinc. A mixture of jealousy and anger simmered inside her at those born on this side of the wall, those who knew nothing of physical work, who only consumed.

Tox hated herself for wanting to be like them, even for a day. But she had to fill that deep ache, told herself that once would be enough, that she'd cherish the memory, replay it every night as she lay shivering and starving on that dirt floor.

The New Hue Automat featured a rainbow screen that repeated the words from the ad, and she swiped her card. Thoughts of the pod she'd saved for disappeared as the limited-time offer popped up on the screen, and she raised a shaking hand to make her selection: the most expensive Hue. It reduced her balance to sixteen credits.

A drawer extended to reveal a silver packet labeled DIANTHUS PINK. She snatched the pouch and hid in the shadows behind the Automats. The label promised twenty-four hours of living as the most coveted of all the Chroma. One just had to swallow the candy within. Below that instruction, it read, WARNING: CONSUMPTION BY LESSERS PUNISHABLE BY DEATH.

Tox tore open the pouch to reveal a clear, glassy orb filled with sparkling pink liquid. She popped the candy in her mouth, and it dissolved, releasing a spray of pure sugar sweeter than even that glorious taste of cotton candy.

Her vision changed first, drenching the world in a rosy glow. The smell of vanilla followed, seeping from every pore. Scalp tingling, she rounded the Automats to peer at her reflection in the silvery surface. Her lank hair sprang into fuchsia spirals, and her lips plumped and deepened in color.

Tox's skin shifted from gray to a shimmering coral, and for the first time in her life, she felt good, light, energetic.

A tinkling giggle slipped from her throat as she spun into the street, dancing under the glow of streetlights.

The next twenty-four hours stretched ahead, her mind spinning with the possibilities of all she could experience. First, she'd use her few precious credits to buy clothes. But before she could take a step toward the Automats, her leg crumpled beneath her, pain crackling through her bones. Tox wilted to the ground, writhing, as her feet solidified and snapped from her ankles in pink-tinged chunks of stone. Next came her fingers and hands. When she opened her mouth to scream, her tongue split and shattered into bits of gravel. Her head fell back, skull cracking on the asphalt.

Punishment by death wasn't a warning, it was a design. They'd engineered New Hue to execute any Lesser who dared dream of a life beyond Lowtown. The syrupy sweetness of her own warped blood choked her throat, then turned to cement, cutting off her last, honey-scented breath.

The repetitive hum of a robotic street cleaner sounded, angling toward the pile of dianthus stones. The machine was programmed to patrol near the Automats, to gather any piles of rock, bits of metal, bunches of rags, or other detritus.

PLAYING TRICKS

DINA HAD NEVER seen her dad cry until the day he left. His face was puffy and wet with tears when he leaned down to kiss her cheek.

"I'll see you soon, okay, Button?"

Dina stared at the scarred wood floor, dark curls shadowing her face. She knew he was lying, having talked to the judge about what he'd called Dina's "home-life" before the judge awarded Mom full custody.

"Just focus on getting well, Greg," Mom said softly. She opened the front door and waited, fiddling with the frayed cuffs of her Grover Elementary PTA sweatshirt.

Outside, birds chirped, and the sun shone down on a kid riding by on his bike. Dina wondered how everything out there could be so normal when everything inside was so wrong. Their neighbor, Susan, stood at the edge of her front stoop, watching. She'd been over just about every day, comforting Mom and saying what a tough woman she was, what a good mom.

Dad shrugged into his flannel pullover, the one that felt so soft on Dina's face when he hugged her, and walked out pulling the large, rolling suitcase they'd bought for their trip to Orlando. They never went to Disney, though. Dad had been too sick.

Her vision blurred, and she swiped at her face, reminding herself what Dad had said. She was a big girl, strong and brave enough to make it through this. But Dina didn't feel brave, she felt scared. For her dad. For her mom. For herself. Everyone at school had seen Dad that day, watched him get dragged from her second-grade classroom.

"Do I have to go to school tomorrow?" Dina asked.

Mom crouched so they were eye to eye. "Mrs. Felton's okay, and I already let the principal and counselor know what's happening, to look out for you."

Dina rubbed her stomach at the thought of all those pitying looks. Why did Mom have to tell everyone?

"I've got a surprise for you. Come on."

Mom led her through the arch off the entryway into the living room, to the khaki sofa that sat against the far wall. The place they all sat while watching movies on weekends, Dina in the middle as the official popcorn holder. It was just the two of them now, sitting side by side on a sofa that seemed too big. The coffee table held a beat-up, dusty shoe box.

"Go ahead, open it."

Dina lifted the lid and peeled back a layer of brittle tissue paper to reveal a doll with auburn ringlets, pursed red lips, and wide green eyes. Dina smiled, lifting the doll from the box.

"She's beautiful."

"Your grandma gave her to me when I was little, and now she's yours."

Dina tucked the doll in the crook of her arm like a baby, smoothing the white lace-edged ruffles of the emerald-colored dress.

Mom hugged her close. "Her name is Pansy, like the flower. Good to squeeze when you're feeling sad. And a great listener, too. If there's anything you want to talk about."

"I love her." Dina leaned into Mom's embrace. There would still be three of them to watch movies together, after all.

PANSY PERCHED ON the corner of the desk that sat beside Dina's twin bed. "It's his favorite color," she said, finishing the blue construction paper card, which she'd cut in the shape of a heart and decorated with stickers.

"Time for bed," Mom said from the doorway.

Dina grabbed Pansy, then realized the doll was over-dressed. "Can we make her some other clothes?" She looked down at her own yellow cotton nightgown, one of several she and Mom had made together. Dina even had her own sewing kit in the desk drawer.

"Sure." Mom picked up the card. "This for Dad?"

"Yeah." Dina crawled into bed, burrowing beneath her floral, down comforter. She tucked Pansy in beside her.

"I'll make sure he gets it." Mom kissed her on the forehead. "Love you."

"Love you, too." Dina watched Mom flip off the light switch and close the door most—but not all—of the way. Footsteps sounded on the wood floor as she walked down the hall to her bedroom.

A night-light plugged in near Dina's bedroom door cast a triangular glow over her bed and across the wall and ceiling. The dim light left the end of the room at the foot of the bed in shadow, and Dina eyed her closet, a single door with wood slats. She hated that closet, which was the perfect place for a monster to hide.

A thump, like something heavy falling, sounded from somewhere in the house. Dina froze, waited for the sound of Dad yelling, of him stomping into her room. But nothing else happened, because he wasn't there anymore.

"Dad isn't bad, he's just sick," she whispered to Pansy. "You weren't around then. Well, I guess you were—up in the attic—but you probably couldn't hear."

Her face heated at the realization she was talking to a toy, treating the doll as if it could understand. But Mom said it was okay to talk to Pansy, and Dina had no one else to tell her secrets.

"At first, Dad thought things were moving, being put in different places, then he swore there was a little girl screaming. He'd come in and pull me out of bed, thinking it was me—that I was being hurt." She hugged Pansy close. "He even came to my school, screaming that he *knew* they were doing something to me. It was really scary. I'm sort of…glad he's gone."

Guilty tears stung her eyes, and she clenched them shut.

A quiet giggle sounded.

Dina gasped and opened her eyes. There wasn't anyone in the doorway, so she stared at the closet. *Could* someone be hiding in there?

The giggle came again, right beside her head.

From Pansy.

But that wasn't possible. Dina stared into the doll's unblinking green eyes. "Pansy?"

"Diiiinaaaa," the doll answered.

Dina yelped and shoved Pansy off the bed. The doll landed on the floor, propped beside the night-light. It lit up the face, made the eyes twinkle with mischief.

Dina squinted, stared at the porcelain face. Her breath wheezed in and out of her lungs. Had the glass eyes moved just a little, rolling in their sockets to stare back up at her?

She yanked the covers over her head in the universal monster-protection strategy. Pansy didn't make any more sounds, and eventually, Dina fell asleep. Her dreams were filled with her father ranting about the moving things, the screaming girl, the nightmares that only he could see and hear.

Mom came in the next morning to wake Dina but stopped at the sight of Pansy on the floor. "What's she doing down there?" she asked Dina. She smoothed the doll's disheveled ringlets.

The story of the giggling, of the doll saying her name, stuck in Dina's throat. It couldn't be real. She had to have imagined it. "I… She fell."

"Silly Pansy." Mom set the doll on the desk.

Pansy didn't laugh or talk, just stared straight ahead, lips pursed in a hint of a smile.

Dina slipped out of her bed on the side farthest from the desk. "I think maybe I'm too old for dolls."

"Who says? Lots of people have dolls, even adults."

The cool air chilled Dina's bare arms and legs, her limbs exposed by the sleeveless nightgown. "You should take her back. She's yours."

Mom frowned. "You don't like her."

"No, I—"

"She's an antique, you know, an expensive one. But you probably want a Barbie or something instead."

Dina crossed her arms as a shiver shook her body.

"I know what this is. You're trying to get back at me for your father." Mom's face flushed red.

"I'm not—"

"Just wait until you get older. You'll understand. Parents have to do hard things sometimes to protect their children. That's what I did. That's what I *had* to do. Before he got worse and hurt one of us."

Dina cringed. "I'm sorry, Mom. I like her. I swear."

"It's okay." Mom's mouth turned down at the corners. "It's just been…a lot lately. And I thought, I don't know, that Pansy could help you like she helped me."

"She will. She does." Dina tried for a smile. "I love her."

DINA LAID IN bed, covers pulled over her head, and tried not to listen to Pansy's whispers. She'd almost gotten used to them over the past two weeks, when every night, after tucking Dina in, Mom placed Pansy on the far corner of the desk and shut off the light.

Not only did the doll whisper and giggle throughout the night, she moved.

By morning, Pansy would be perched on the edge of the desk closest to the bed or lying beside Dina on top of the covers. This morning, Dina opened her eyes to find Pansy lying on the pillow, just an inch away.

Dina shrieked and shoved the doll.

Pansy struck the wall with a thump and fell face-down on the floor.

"Leave me alone!" Dina screamed, pressing her fists over her eyes.

Mom rushed into the room. "Are you all right?"

Dina uncovered her face to see Mom stooping to pick up the doll.

"Again with this? You know, Pansy is precious to me. You treating her like this… It's mean and hurtful."

Dina sniffled. "I'm sorry. I tried. I really did. But I can't stand it."

Mom sat on the edge off the bed, still clutching the doll by one tiny hand. "What are you talking about? Tried what?"

"Pansy. I tried to be her friend, but she won't leave me alone."

Mom's eyes narrowed. "Leave you alone? What in the world do you mean?"

A sob hitched in Dina's chest. "She talks to me."

"Oh, hon, that's just your imagination."

"No. She talks and laughs, and she moves. Even climbs into my bed. I don't like her doing that."

Pansy slipped from Mom's hand and fell to the floor.

"Oh, no. No, no, no," said Mom. She stood and rushed from the room.

"Mom?"

The silence stretched out until Dina couldn't stand it any longer. She scrambled out of bed, gave the doll a wide berth, and raced down the hall in pursuit.

She found Mom in the kitchen. The blinds were still closed, blocking the morning sun and making the normally cheery room appear cave-like. Mom was slumped on a stool at the kitchen island, phone pressed firmly to her ear.

"She thinks the fucking doll is moving, Greg!"

Dina halted, the F-word freezing her in place like a slap.

"I know that." Mom quieted for a minute. "No, you didn't see her… It's like before. When it first started with you." She whispered that last sentence.

Dina took a step back, considered running back to her room. But it wasn't safe. Not with Pansy there.

Mom stood and thrust the phone at Dina. "Talk to your father."

Hand trembling, Dina reached out and took the phone. "D-Dad?"

"Hi, Button. I miss you."

"I miss you, too." Dina turned her back to Mom.

"Tell me about Pansy."

"I don't want to," she whispered.

"It's okay. I'm not mad. Just tell me what's happening."

This sounded like the old dad she remembered, the one who was so patient, always had time to listen to her problems.

"Okay." She told him everything. When she finished, there was only silence. "Dad?"

"I'm here." He sighed. "I know this all seems real to you."

"It *is* real!"

"Hush now and listen."

"Okay," she mumbled.

"I hear and see things, too, sometimes. Or I used to."

"I know."

"I was imagining things that weren't real."

Dina remembered him shoving her teacher Mrs. Felton to the ground, breaking her arm. "You were sick."

"Yeah, I was sick. I *am* sick. But I'm getting help, taking medicine to get better."

"Are you coming home?"

"Not quite yet, button. Soon, I hope."

"I miss you, Dad."

"I miss you, too, so very much."

She swallowed; her throat tight.

"The thing about my sickness is it sometimes runs in families—" He cleared his throat, and she wondered if he might be trying not to cry, too. "Well, it might be that I gave it to you."

"I feel fine."

"This is a different kind of sickness, one in your head. But the doctors can see, and they can help. Like they're helping me."

Legs suddenly weak, she dropped to the floor and drew her knees to her chest. "Am I gonna have to leave, too? Live somewhere else?"

"No, no. You just need to see the doctor. Tell them what you told me."

"I don't want to."

"They'll help you. I promise. You trust your dad, don't you?"

"Yeah." And she did, even after everything.

"Then I need you to do this for me so you can get better, too, and we can all be together again. Okay? Promise?"

Dina did want her dad back, her real one from before. She wanted them to be a family again. "I promise."

DINA WATCHED AS Mom placed Pansy in the shoe box and climbed the ladder into the attic, returned the doll to its place among the dusty totes of old clothes and forgotten toys. Dina didn't follow, because the pills the doctor had given her made her head fuzzy and her knees wobbly, and climbing would have been difficult.

She tried to forget about the doll as she sat coloring at the coffee table, but Mom and her PTA friends wouldn't stop whispering about Dina and her imagination. They all clustered around the kitchen island, taking turns hugging Mom and murmuring words of sympathy and encouragement.

That night, Dina lay awake, too frightened to sleep. Not because of Pansy, but because she didn't want to be sick. Mom and Dr. Vicki said it would be fine, that she would get better. But what if she got worse, like Dad? What if Mom sent her away, too?

A whisper sounded, and Dina bolted upright, heart thumping. She strained to hear, but the only noise was the soft whoosh of the air conditioning. Had she mistaken it for a whisper? She cataloged her room, and everything seemed to be in its proper place, nothing there that shouldn't be. The door was still cracked open, displaying a slice of the dark hallway.

The sound came again, definitely a whisper, saying "Diiiinaaaa" from beneath her bed.

Gripping the edge of the comforter so tight her fingers ached, she reminded herself that she was strong and brave. And if this was her imagination, the medicine would help. She leaned over the side of the bed, lowering herself until she could see past the dust ruffle. Her eyes took a moment to decipher the small, dark shape on the floor.

Pansy, lying on her back, her head facing Dina.

Pansy, giggling.

Dina yelped and pulled herself back up, yanking the covers over her head and lying as flat as she could. Tears leaked from her eyes and soaked her pillow. She'd seen Mom pack up the doll and return the box to the attic. How could Pansy be back?

Dr. Vicki's words came back to Dina. "Sometimes the mind plays tricks."

The air left her lungs in a whoosh. Could she be imagining Pansy like Dad had imagined things moving? The thought made her cry harder, sobs wracking her chest until, exhausted from fear, she fell asleep.

The next morning, Pansy was gone, and Dina thought maybe the doll had never been there at all.

That night at bedtime, Dina took the pill Mom gave her, even though it made her feel dizzy. She didn't want to see things that weren't real.

"Can you check under the bed?" she asked.

Mom raised her eyebrows. "Aren't you a little old to be scared of monsters?"

"Can you just check?"

She wasn't sure what she hoped for. If the doll *was* there, it meant she wasn't imagining it, wasn't making it up. She didn't know it that was worse.

Mom knelt beside the bed. "Nothing under here but the dust bunnies."

Dina blinked away the itchiness in her eyes.

"Love you." Mom flipped off the overhead light.

"Love you, too," Dina managed.

She lay there, staring at the ceiling, trying not to think about her mind being sick. About everyone at school finding out. She reminded herself of her friend Sam, who had diabetes, and how he had to take medicine *and* stick his finger each day. So, taking a pill wasn't so bad. People got sick all the time, and they took medicine for it. That's what Dr. Vicki said, and Dad, too.

Feeling marginally better, she sunk into a restless sleep.

A noise ripped her from her nightmares sometime later, and she sucked in a panicked breath. "Please, not again," she prayed, holding perfectly still.

"Diiiinaaaa," came the whisper from under the bed.

"You're not here. You're not real."

A giggle sounded.

Dina closed her eyes tight. "Leave me alone."

Another giggle.

She pulled her covers over her head as she had the night before, intending to pretend Pansy didn't exist. She wished Dad could hug her back to sleep. But if he were there, she knew he'd tell her to face her problems. Just telling yourself things weren't happening didn't work.

Dina had to know if the doll was real or just her imagination, had to *prove* it.

She threw off her comforter and leaned over to grab her crafting scissors from the desk, then dangled her feet over the edge of the bed. Her toes twitched in anticipation of the tiny doll's hands grasping her ankles.

After several deep breaths, she slipped off the edge of the bed and knelt on the floor.

Pansy laid in the same spot.

Before Dina could lose her nerve, she snaked an arm under the bed and grabbed the doll by the skirt to tug it closer. Pulse pounding in her ears like a drum, Dina snipped a piece of lace ruffle off with her scissors.

Pansy giggled.

Dina yelped and shoved the doll back under the bed, scrambling onto the mattress and under the covers, scissors still clutched in one hand and the snip of fabric in the other.

Pansy was gone when Dina woke, but she still had the scrap of lace tucked in her fist. She had proof. Her mind wasn't playing tricks, Pansy was.

Dina knew about evil doll monsters; she'd seen *Child's Play* at a sleepover. She thought about telling Mom but knew she wouldn't believe it, not without the doll as proof. Even with the doll, she'd probably think Dina had retrieved Pansy from the attic as a way to sell the hoax.

She had to be brave. She had to catch Pansy and stop her for good.

DINA WAS TENSE, her body as rigid as a board when Mom tucked her in that night.

"You okay?" Mom asked.

"Fine." Dina resisted the urge to check under her pillow for the knife she'd stolen from the kitchen, knowing her dull-tipped scissors wouldn't be enough to defeat an evil doll.

"Maybe I should look under the bed again, just to be safe." Mom checked beneath the bed, declared the space empty of monsters, and then said good night.

After Mom left, Dina counted to two hundred, stuffed a pillow beneath the covers to take her place, and climbed out of bed. With knife in hand, she crept toward the closet, gripped the knob, and flung open the door.

Empty of monsters.

Easing out a relieved breath, she stepped inside the closet, stood with her back to her hanging clothes, and closed the door so that she could peek through the wood slats in the door. She waited for over an hour, had to switch the knife from her right hand to her left, then back again, to wipe her sweaty palms. Dina yawned and blinked rapidly, trying to stave off tiredness. Just when she thought Pansy wasn't coming, the floorboards in the hallway creaked.

She froze, gripped the knife tight.

The door edged open another foot, blocking her view, and Dina held her breath. She watched the bottom edge of the door, waiting for Pansy to come walking, or maybe crawling, into the room. But the figure that entered was much taller.

Mom. Probably coming to check on Dina, to make sure she was okay. She was lucky to have such a good Mom, knew not everyone did. But if she checked the bed, she'd only find pillows. Dina would be in big trouble if she were found in the closet with a knife. Mom might even think she was going to hurt herself or someone else, like Dad.

But Mom didn't touch the mound of pillows. She knelt on the floor, something in her hands.

Pansy.

Dina slapped one hand over her mouth and watched as Mom slid the doll beneath the bed before standing and leaving the room, closing the door most of the way behind her. The floorboards creaked beneath her retreating footsteps.

Feeling dazed, as if she might be dreaming, Dina exited her hiding place in the closet. She dragged Pansy out from beneath the bed and sat on the floor with the doll in her lap. Pansy giggled, and Dina jumped, her heart galloping in her chest. This was no dream.

Putting down the knife, she held the doll's mouth to her ear and waited. Another giggle, but not from the mouth. More from the chest. Frowning, Dina flipped the doll over and unfastened the back of its dress to display the soft body beneath. A line of pristine, white stitches ran down Pansy's spine.

Hand trembling, Dina cut through the stitches to the stuffing beneath. Something hard and black was wedged within the torso, and she tore it free. The slim, square, plastic box had a waffle pattern on one side and a battery cover and switch on the other. When Pansy started giggling again, Dina flipped the switch to silence the voice.

Her stomach clenched in a tight knot as she pushed the doll from her lap to lay limp on the floor, no more possessed than any of her toys. She got up and braced herself on the footboard while a wave of dizziness passed. When she felt sure she could walk, she crept from her room and down the hall, staying close to the wall to avoid the creaking floorboards.

She reached Mom's closed bedroom door and pressed her ear to the wood. From within the room came a high-pitched giggle, then a soft, "Diiiinaaaa."

It hadn't been Dina's mind or Pansy playing tricks.

Mom had been making her hear voices, had been moving the doll.

Clamping her mouth closed on the scream that wanted to escape, Dina crept backward, away from Mom's room. Icy fingers of fear gripped Dina's lungs and squeezed them tight at the realization the monster wasn't under the bed or in the closet, but in the next bedroom.

Nightgown soaked through and clinging to her sweat-slicked skin, Dina crawled back into bed, bringing Pansy and the speaker with her. Working carefully in the dim light, she turned the speaker on, placed it back inside the doll, repaired the stitches with her sewing kit, and returned poor Pansy to her hiding place.

Dina lay in bed, a painful lump clogging her throat. She'd thought Mom loved her, would always take care of her. Her chin trembled, and a sob hitched in her chest.

A soft giggle sounded, and her sadness evaporated.

Mom had *made* Dina think she was sick. Probably Dad, too. She wasn't a good mom at all. She was mean and bad and a liar. But Dina was brave and strong, and she knew how to stop monsters.

She reached beneath her pillow and gripped the knife. When Mom came to move Pansy, Dina would be ready.

SORRY, WE'RE OPEN

THE HOLE IN the Wall bar is the oldest in town and the smallest. It occupies the corner of an historic red-brick building next to an alley, and the sign that hangs on the door says, "Sorry, We're Open." Though I'm standing outside on the sidewalk, waiting for the right moment to enter, I know exactly what's inside. A bar top with five barstools takes up half the room. The other half holds three small tables and a partition wall that forms a makeshift hallway leading to two bathrooms where your knees touch the wall if you dare sit. The room smells of stale beer, sweat, and death. I might be the only one that can smell that last one, which is like breathing the dust of crushed autumn leaves until you choke.

The ceiling is quite high, tall enough to hold two people stacked atop one another and then some, which allows for maximum display space. Every inch of the walls, even behind the bar, is covered with memorabilia. Neon bar signs and tin art, as you'd expect, but also bumper stickers, photos, drawings, license plates, bicycle parts, stuffed animals, Christmas ornaments, Mardi Gras beads, and more. Just to the right, as you step in the door, a bright yellow bumper sticker with black writing says, *Jesus is Coming, Look Busy.* When she was alive, it was Hope's favorite.

I asked once about the framed photos, which range from very old black and white to Polaroid to digital, but none of the bartenders or bouncers know anyone captured in the stills. A grinning man holding a fish, a bunch of kids in Halloween masks, a woman in a corseted dress standing beside a horse, a couple in the middle of a kiss, an old piano not being played—to name a few. No one appears in the photos more than once, either. We checked one night. Hope craned her head to examine each one while I listed what she called out on a bar napkin with my felt pen. That napkin is now tucked into the neck bow of a stuffed lavender bunny near the ceiling. I don't know how it got there.

The bumper stickers seem to multiply, and I discover a new one every night. *My Kid Beat Up Your Honor Student, ZAPPA for President, Only Users Lose Drugs, Life is a Banquet So Eat Me,* and on and on. They curl at the edges, pull away from the wall, and are covered with splatters of beer and layers of dust. Nothing is ever taken down, so they are layers deep, new stickers overlaying the old.

The bathrooms are painted Pepto-Bismol pink and covered in markered graffiti. Toasts and greetings and declarations of love cover the walls. Our favorite toast was *Here's to the men we love, here's to the men that love us, and if the men we love don't love us, fuck them and here's to us.* I say "was" because every so often they repaint the bathroom, always that same pink, and that toast is invisible now, just like Hope.

Most nights the bar is busy. It's a college town, and they sell dollar-fifty Jell-O shots. The chatter of drunk people fills the space and spills out the door into the street, but it won't drown out Hope's scream, though no one hears that but me.

The far table against the partition wall was ours—hers and mine—when she was alive. We'd out-wait anyone occupying the spot, sometimes buying them Jell-O shots as a bribe, and swoop in to claim our corner. Now, the table is just mine. If anyone is sitting there when I walk in, they're asked to move. The bartenders look out for me, make sure I have my spot to sit and a beer to drink. People often ask to borrow to the empty chair, but I tell them it's taken.

I catch the looks the employees exchange, the pity in their eyes when they see me, but I'm not the only one they look at that way. I didn't realize it while Hope was alive, but bars are very sad places filled with people trying too hard to have fun, trying too hard to forget, and trying too hard to kill themselves, albeit slowly. They're also the perfect hunting ground. They turn people into prey.

We never fought and always stuck together, until that night, the night that took Hope's life and ruined mine forever. She'd met a hot guy with dark, wavy hair and kind brown eyes who joined us at our corner table and didn't hesitate to pay for both our drinks. The more they talked, moving closer to one another and shrinking into their own little world, the angrier I got. We never left one another alone at the bar and had an agreement that when one of us wanted to go, we went. But that night, she stayed.

I stalked off to our apartment, only a five-minute walk, leaving her with him. When an hour passed with no response to my texts, I went back. Last call just passed, the crowds on the sidewalk had thinned, only the most dedicated partiers remained. I was standing in the doorway to the bar, scanning the dwindling crowd, when I heard her scream, a short shriek cut off so quickly it could have been imagined. By the time I rounded the corner to the alley, it was too late.

The alarm on my phone buzzes, signaling 1:30 a.m. Last call. Sucking in a deep breath, I ready myself to see Hope.

JAMES IS ON duty tonight, working the door. A tall guy who wears a beanie no matter the weather. He smiles and waves me in without checking my ID. I think of Hope. No matter how often we came to the bar, she always got carded and complained that no one ever remembered her. I would laugh and insist that I was jealous because she could easily become a spy and would likely be recruited by the CIA soon.

Now she's stuck in this place where no one remembers her, not really. Except me.

A group of tipsy college girls in matching sorority tees stand against the bar top and raise a round of pink Jell-O shots, probably watermelon, high in the air to cheers. Two guys stand off to the side, eyeing the sorority group. I almost stop, tell the girls to watch out for themselves, but I've had that conversation many times, and I only get looked at like a freak and told to leave them alone.

My table in the back corner is occupied by a guy and girl who are actively groping one another. But the bartender, Tonya of the horn-rimmed glasses, sees me coming. She edges out from behind the bar with two shots. Leaning over the couple, she points to the middle table, then moves over to set down her offering. They immediately vacate my spot to grab their free drinks.

"Thanks," I say as I pass her.

"No problem, hon."

I slide into the wobbly chair that faces the wall and leave the other two seats open. Tonya sets a beer in front of me, and I almost grab her hand to try to apologize for what comes next, to explain, but I don't know how.

Music filters through the talk and laughter of the bar's patrons: "She Talks to Angels" by The Black Crows. The chill of my glass moves up my hand, my arm, seems to encase my whole body. Trembling, I take several big swallows, finishing half my drink.

Two girls stumble out from behind the partition wall that hides the bathrooms, supporting one another. They kiss, laugh, and stumble on. I avert my eyes, feel the heat rushing up my neck and face at the memory of our kiss. The night before I lost her, Hope and I had squeezed ourselves into that tiny bathroom, our shins pressed against the toilet bowl as we debated what to mark on the graffiti-covered pink wall.

"We have to write something really good," she said, grabbing my shoulders.

"Totally," I said in my mock serious voice, mirroring her pose. Our faces were inches apart.

She met my eyes, then looked down, her chin-length hair curtaining her face. "How about Hope Loves Emi?"

"*Does* Hope Love Emi?" My chest tightened.

"Well…yeah." She gave a hesitant smile.

Swallowing, I said, "Emi Loves Hope, too." Then I leaned in and touched my lips to hers, tentatively at first.

She drew me closer, kissed me back. Her mouth tasted like mint and beer and Doritos.

We broke apart after a moment, both of us giggling, our faces flushed. Later that night, she would say we couldn't let that happen ever again.

The alarm on my phone buzzes, bringing me back to the present, and I eye the screen. A countdown clock appears, starting at one hundred. I tip back the rest of my beer, place the empty glass on the table, and put my hand in my hoodie pocket, clutching the knife's hilt.

A tremor starts in my bones, threatening to splinter my resolve. When the timer reaches zero, the lights in the bar flicker, and I watch a figure appear in one of the empty chairs across from me. The handsome façade, with the seemingly kind brown eyes, is marred by a jagged wound that runs vertical down the neck. His mouth twists into a sneer, the same expression I saw when I rounded the corner of the alley that night. Pinning Hope against the brick building with his body, his knife had flashed in the moonlight as he drew it across her throat. I had cried out her name, and when he turned, he let her wilt to the ground.

He came at me, brandishing the blade covered in Hope's blood, while she flailed on the grimy concrete behind him, gasping for air and desperately trying to seal the wound with her hands. I raised my arms to block the knife, but the blow never came. Hope had grabbed his pant leg, clutched the fabric, caused him to stumble. When he looked back, I lunged at him, grabbed his knife-hand, and drove the blade into his neck.

Sitting across from me now, in the same spot where he'd seduced Hope, he grins as if we're friends sharing a drink. Hope materializes in the chair beside him, her shoulders sagging, and her head hanging low.

"Hope, it's me, Emi," I whisper, willing her to look up. She used to see me, used to try to talk.

He reaches over and strokes her face. She doesn't react, don't even flinch.

"Let her go! Now!" Attacking him won't work. It does no good and would only result in James removing me from the bar, as he's done many times before.

The monster shakes his head and drops his hand from her cheek to her neck, his thumb resting in the gaping wound that killed her. She slumps there, a marionette whose strings have been cut.

"Emi loves Hope," I say, knowing I have to go after her before there's nothing left of the girl I love.

My hand trembles as I pull the knife from my pocket and fold it open, staring at the blade hidden in shadow beneath the table. The only way to save her is to follow, to go after her before she's gone forever. I planned for this moment, rehearsed in my mind the quick swipe of the razor-sharp blade across my jugular, but my hand won't move from my lap.

Tears sting my eyes and spill down my face.

I press the tip of blade into the pad of my thumb, feel the sharp pain of the tiny cut and watch as a dot of red blooms on my skin. A sob hitches in my chest.

A full beer appears in front of me as Tonya says, "Last call, hon," before sidling back behind the bar.

I fold the knife closed, shove it back in my pocket, and wrap my hands around the chilled glass. Sucking in a deep, shaky breath, I look up. The chairs across from me are empty.

ANTIFREEZE AND SWEET PEAS

GRANDMA KAY'S BAKERY opened at precisely 6:00 a.m., and the first customer entered, sending the bell above the door jingling and letting the smell of buttery pastries waft out into the street to tempt the dozen or so patrons waiting in line. The store had a European charm, with only enough space for customers to enter one at a time, where they could peer directly into the glass-covered display cases without trouble.

Five years prior, Grandma Kay—bless her heart—had passed away quietly in the night, necessitating that her granddaughter, Delilah, continue things. Delilah had been kneading dough with Grandma since the day she could walk, so it was natural for her to take the bakery over. The position was a blessing, a way to live out her true calling while also providing a stable life for her daughter.

"Morning, Bill. The usual?" Delilah asked, dusting off her floury hands on her apron.

He nodded. "Morning, darlin.'" Bill was a good man. Not tainted, like some of them.

Delilah slid the already packed box of dinner rolls across the counter, then placed a single, paper-wrapped chocolate croissant on top. "On the house." She winked.

"Well, I don't think the missus would approve." His cheeks pinked as he held out a ten-dollar bill.

Delilah took his money. "It'll be our secret, then." Just as it was every week.

"Keep the change. And tell that little Sweet Pea of yours the missus is lookin' for summer help at the diner if she's interested."

"I'll let her know." She dropped his change in the jar by the till. "Thanks, sugar." A summer job might be just the thing to keep Sweet Pea out of trouble until school started. She'd sure been pushing the limits lately by staying out past her curfew with her new boyfriend, Adam.

The bell jingled as Bill exited and Mrs. Parsons entered. She started to angle through the door, but a man in a sharp-looking suit and tie pushed past her.

"Hey, man, there's a line," someone called out, earning mumbles of agreement from his cohorts.

The man in the suit ignored the comment and left Mrs. Parsons outside glaring at the closed door. He stared down at his phone, tapping at the screen with fingers coated in blood that smeared the device and dripped from his wrists to pool on the floor. Blood only Delilah could see.

She'd screamed and screamed the night she saw Daddy's hands stained with death. Now she was used to it, welcomed the sight as a blessed gift from God himself.

She smiled. "What can I get you?"

"One minute," the man said without looking up.

"Of course, sir." Her voice was as sweet as powdered sugar.

He gave a cocksure smirk and stuck his phone back in his pocket, leaving a bloody smear on his perfectly tailored jacket. "You don't look like a Grandma Kay."

She laughed, low and throaty, with a hint that it was just for him, then leaned forward to give him an eyeful of cleavage. "Delilah." She offered her hand.

He took her hand in his stained fingers and leaned down to place a kiss on the back of her hand. "I'm Charles."

She extracted herself from his grip and did not wipe her hand on her apron, as much as she would have liked to. "Pleased to meet you, Charles. What can I get you?"

"A dozen assorted pastries, for my office." He straightened his tie.

Oh, yes, you are such an important man, she thought, her lips ticking up at the corners. She packed the pastries in a box and set them on the counter. "I've got something special for you."

Delilah stepped through the door to the kitchen and keyed in the combo on the small locking cooler in the corner. She took a fruit tart, one topped with sour oranges and sweet blueberries, from the rack of her special pastries, those reserved for her murdering bastards.

She wrapped the pastry in paper and returned to Charles.

"For you." She placed a red lipsticked kiss on the paper. "Don't go sharing it with anyone else, okay sugar?"

He made sort of a growling sound in the back of his throat, a predatory gleam in his eye. He unwrapped the tart and took a bite. "Mmm."

"That'll be $26.67, sugar." One bite and she knew he was hooked. He'd keep coming back again and again.

DELILAH FLIPPED THE sign to "Closed" and slumped against the door, exhaustion pulling at her body. She'd have loved nothing more than to climb the spiral staircase at the rear of the kitchen, up to their loft apartment, and collapse on the sofa for an evening of reality TV.

But her work wasn't done…yet.

She gathered the excess cash and checks from the till and shook her head at the little handwritten note Charles had jotted on the back of his business card: *Call me* and a phone number.

Yeah, right. Who knew if his last conquest had even survived the encounter?

Delilah prepared the bank deposit, then made her way through the bakery and into the industrial kitchen. She baked most of her pastries in the early morning, but her special batch required extra care, so she made them the night before.

Her satellite radio sat at the end of the metal prep table, and she flipped it to the Tom Jones station, in honor of her mama. Delilah closed her eyes and swayed back and forth to the music, like Mama used to do. With a smile that could melt the heart of the most stubborn old grump, folks said Mama was an angel come to life. She always said Delilah was her little cherub from heaven.

Delilah figured God was so upset at what became of his angel, he'd blessed Delilah with the sight.

She mixed flour, salt, butter, and ice water by hand on the flour-dusted work surface, then split the dough into twelve equal parts. The process of slowly poisoning the men took months, and her current group had grown to nine. She'd stopped questioning why these particular men—and it was always men—were attracted to her, to the bakery. Just figured that God had made her the flame, and the men were the unsuspecting moths begging to get burnt.

After retrieving the mortar and pestle and her electronic scale, she pulled the pill bottle from her apron pocket. Tom Jones sang "She's a Lady" as Delilah sprinkled several pills into the mortar and crushed them into powder. She spread the dough balls out on the table and pressed a divot in each ball with her thumb. Using the scale, she carefully weighed out equal doses of Xanax. Those who received her special tarts felt intense euphoria after eating one and always came back for more. Just a little something extra to up the attraction.

The bell in the bakery jingled, and Delilah froze.

"Hey, Mom." Pea entered the kitchen, already sinking her teeth into one of the few remnants from the display case, a blueberry Danish.

Delilah dusted her hands off on her apron and rounded the prep table. "No track practice today, Sweet Pea?"

"Canceled." Pea tried for a scowl, but her face couldn't quite manage it. "And it's Penny, Mom. I told you I'm too old for that nickname."

Ever since Pea started her senior year, she'd gotten in her head she was a grown up. "Doesn't matter how old you are, you'll always be my Sweet Pea."

"Just don't call me that in front of my friends."

"We'll see." Delilah leaned close to collect a blueberry flavored kiss on the cheek from her daughter.

"What're you doing?" Pea eyed the balls of dough.

"Just making a couple things for a special order." Delilah moved to block Pea's view of her creations.

"You mean the ones you keep all locked up?" Pea grinned and rubbed her hands together. "You've got to teach me your secret recipes sometime. I'll help."

"No." Not ever. Delilah put her arm over her daughter's shoulders and steered her toward the back of the kitchen. "I printed a couple more college brochures and left them for you on the desk. Why don't you go take a look and see if you want to add any of them to the list to visit?"

"You know, most parents are happy when their kids want to follow in their footsteps."

Delilah's throat tightened at the thought. "I just don't want you to miss out, hon. You've got so much potential."

"You have to say that. Besides, Adam is staying here, and I don't want to be too far away from him."

"You've only been dating for a month, and I haven't even met him yet. Give it some time." Delilah clenched her teeth. The last thing she wanted was for her daughter to take after her and end up pregnant at nineteen, with nowhere to go but back to the bakery.

"I'll bring him for dinner next week, okay?" Pea gripped the straps of her backpack. "If you just give him a chance, you'll see he's good for me."

"We'll talk about it later. Go on upstairs. I'll be done soon, and we can figure out dinner."

"Fine." Pea exhaled in frustration and stomped up the staircase. Very adult-like.

Once Delilah heard the television blasting above her in the loft, she returned to her recipe. She opened the cupboard beneath the sink and retrieved the bottle of antifreeze from the back—one of the brands that didn't add a bitter flavor to disguise the naturally sweet taste.

After adding a teaspoon of the liquid to each ball of dough, Delilah donned rubber gloves and kneaded the dough until the ingredients were evenly mixed. She molded the portions into individual tart pans, then popped them in the oven. After topping with a bit of vanilla custard, she'd finish with luscious strawberries, raspberries, and blackberries.

Her murdering men would gobble them right up.

A WEEK LATER, Anthony entered the bakery just after eight in the morning, his face pale and unshaven, his eyes sunken, and his normally pressed transit uniform wrinkled and smelling unwashed.

Delilah mimicked a worried expression. "Oh, sugar, you don't look so good."

A hacking cough wracked his body, and he raised one blood-stained hand to cover his mouth. "I wouldn't miss breakfast with you." He left a smear of red across his mouth, like a twisted circus clown. "Since Linda left me, you're the best part of my day."

Linda "ran off" at the same time the blood appeared on his hands. When Delilah first began acting on her sight, she'd investigated the men first, made sure they were guilty. Every single one proved to be a murderer. Now she simply accepted her visions as truth.

"I've got exactly what you need." Delilah stepped into the kitchen and retrieved three beautiful peach-and-kiwi tarts from the cooler, slipping them into a paper bag. After months of eating her treats every day, his body was going into organ failure. Just a few more of her special pastries and he'd be dead in the grave.

"What's that?" Pea asked.

Delilah slammed the cooler shut and spun to face her daughter. "What are you doing up so early on a Saturday?"

"Meeting Stephanie for spin class." Pea raised her eyebrows. "Another special order?"

"Um, sort of." Delilah folded the bag closed and swallowed to wet her throat. "Will you be back for lunch?"

Pea shrugged. "Maybe. I'll text you." She headed into the bakery.

Delilah followed, gripping the top of the pastry bag.

"Hey, Mr. Watkins." Pea frowned. "Are you okay?"

Anthony swayed slightly, and Delilah rushed around the counter to steady him. "Anthony isn't feeling well, hon." Delilah guided him to the door. She lowered her voice. "Now, I want you to go straight home and eat every pastry in this bag, then get some rest."

"Gotta get to work." He broke into another coughing fit.

Delilah opened the door and walked out with him, trying to get out of Pea's earshot. "You've got sick days, don't ya? Use one." She gave Anthony a stern look and handed him the bag.

He reached in and pulled out a tart, his eyes closing momentarily as he took a bite. His mouth still full and crumbs dotting his lips, he said, "Guess I can take one day off."

"Remember what I said, sugar. Eat those, then straight to bed."

He mumbled an agreement and set off down the street, drifting side to side, unable to walk a straight line. Anyone else would have called a doctor, but her men didn't.

She knew he wouldn't be back tomorrow. He'd be found dead in his home, just like all the others. She'd get a bit jumpy the week after, watching and waiting for the police to knock on her bakery door, but they never did. God watched over His angels.

And there would be one less murderer on the street, one less chance another woman would get hurt.

Mama's face flashed through Delilah's mind, gasping for breath, eyes wide with panic. Delilah had tried to stop Daddy from squeezing Mama's neck, but he'd swatted her away like she weighed nothing. Mama went rag-doll limp. Her head lolled to the side, and she stared right at Delilah.

Daddy sat back, just looked at her mama lying there. "Why do you make me hurt you? Why?" he'd said, his voice cracking on each word.

Then the blood came, coating his hands like he'd dipped them in a bucket of guts. But he hadn't cut Mama or broken her skin. Even though she was only nine years old, Delilah knew that was death-blood on her daddy's hands. Delilah wailed as if she were dying herself, but Daddy never looked at her, not until she got the kitchen knife and stabbed him in the throat.

She'd known she had to do it. For Mama.

In the years since, Delilah had used her knife again and again, but she had to be careful. She couldn't afford to get caught, couldn't risk Sweet Pea. The tarts were better. Cleaner. Safer. Slower. More painful.

"Good morning, beautiful."

The voice wrenched her from her thoughts. "Charles," she said.

He'd parked his Bentley in the loading zone directly in front of the shop. He strutted toward her, dressed in a yuppie's weekend wear: designer jeans, black loafers, and a button up shirt. "Delilah." He said her name like she belonged to him.

He'd been back every day since they met, as she'd known he would. Her treats always hooked them, as did her other…assets. Most of her men were lecherous perverts, after all. "Come on in, sugar."

He pulled open the bakery door in a show of chivalry, and Delilah stepped inside, brushing past him.

Pea was bent over, snagging a croissant from the display case. She stood and hitched her gym bag over her shoulder.

Charles's gaze skipped between the two women. "Wow. I think I'm seeing double." He licked his lips, and Delilah could practically see the fantasy skipping through his mind. "Who's this?"

"My daughter, Sweet Pea." Delilah swallowed down the nausea that wanted to take hold. "Hon, this is Charles."

"It's Penny." She pulled her phone from her pocket and checked the screen. "God, I'm running so late. Steph's going to flip."

"Let me just finish this and box up the order for Mrs. Murray, then I can take you."

"Thanks, Mom. I'll wait in the car." Pea nodded to Charles. "Nice to meet you."

"My pleasure." Charles watched Pea's rear end a little too closely as she pushed out the door.

Delilah slammed her hand down on the counter, a little too hard, so as to draw his attention back to her. "Now, what can I get you today, sugar?"

"I'd love one of your special pastries, if you have any left." He leaned one elbow on the counter.

"For you, I've got two." Delilah hoped her lips formed a smile and not a sneer.

She retrieved the tarts, half hoping he would choke on them, and sent Charles on his lecherous way.

Delilah had just finished wrapping up two dozen brioche buns for Mrs. Murray when her phone gave three quick buzzes from the pocket of her apron. Sweet Pea's ring. Delilah pulled out her phone and checked the waiting text message.

Don't worry about the ride. Charles said he'd take me.

The phone slipped from Delilah's fingers and smacked the tile floor.

A loud buzzing filled her ears, drowned out everything around her as she rushed through the bakery and out onto the street. Charles's car was gone and so was Sweet Pea.

"No, no, no."

Delilah raced back up the steps and into the bakery, slipped and fell as she skittered past the counter. Sprawled on the floor, she snatched up her phone and stared at Sweet Pea's message, now a shattered mosaic in the cracked screen.

The bell above the door jingled.

"We're closed!" Delilah shouted. "Get out of here!"

The bell jingled again.

Her fingers trembled as she pressed the call button.

Ring. Ring. Ring.

"Answer, dammit."

Ring. Ring. Ring.

"You've reached Penny's phone. Leave a message."

"Honey, you need to get away from Charles right now. Please, call me back." Delilah ended the call and immediately started typing out a message.

Get out of that car right now.

Delilah called again. Voicemail.

When her phone finally buzzed in response, a relieved cry jumped from her mouth.

Calm down, Mom. I'm fine.

"Shit!" Delilah got to her feet and paced the kitchen, horrific visions filling her mind. A beautiful girl lying dead on the floor. A man standing above her, his hands dripping blood. But it wasn't a memory of her mother. This time it was Pea, and Delilah just let it happen. She didn't save her baby.

DELILAH SPED DOWN the winding private drive and screeched to a stop next to Charles's Bentley. She stared up at the sprawling Colonial. She'd tracked her daughter's phone here, to what had to be Charles's home. Tears blurred Delilah's eyes, and she swiped them away with the back of her hand as she stared at Pea's last message.

Please just trust me, Mom. I can take care of myself.

Nothing since. All Delilah's calls and texts went unanswered. But she couldn't assume the worst. Her daughter was smart, resourceful. Pea could still be okay. Still be alive.

Delilah faltered. Should she have called the police? Pea wasn't officially missing long enough for them to care, and she couldn't explain how she knew Charles was a killer.

No. She had to take care of this herself, like she always did.

Delilah grabbed the butcher knife from the seat beside her and jumped from her car to run up the front steps of the house. She raised her fist to bang on the sturdy front door, only to find it cracked open.

She pushed the door and let it swing wide, then silently stepped inside.

Sweet Pea's name wanted to leap from her tongue in a scream, but she bit it back. She had to be patient, sneak up on the bastard.

The entry opened to a living room that resembled a modern art museum, all white walls, metal accents, and expensive modernist paintings of shapes. The sofa had been shoved at an angle, and a standing lamp lay broken on the floor.

If Charles had hurt Pea …

Delilah would make him beg for death.

She continued toward an open archway that led into another room.

Once inside, her breath froze in her lungs.

A man was crouched in the center of the dining room, his back to her. The table and chairs had been pushed to the side, and blood was spreading across the wood floor in front of him. He reached into a plastic bucket by his side and pulled out a sponge. He squeezed it until a pinkish liquid poured out.

Delilah was too late.

Every sound muted except for the pounding of her own heart in her ears. Memories of her father crouched over her mother's body flickered in her vision, the past superimposing itself on the present.

A shriek erupted from her throat as she propelled herself across the room.

The man turned just before she reached him, his eyes wide as she tackled him to the floor, pressed his back to the pool of blood. Sweet Pea's blood.

Her vision narrowed on the man's face. The man who had hurt her baby girl. Straddling his body, she raised her knife.

"Wait! Stop!" He held up his hands to claim innocence.

Not Charles. This face was more boy than man.

She hesitated.

He grabbed at her wrists, and his blood-coated fingers slid over her skin.

Stomach acid stung her throat. Murderer. He was a murderer.

She yanked free of his grip and pressed her knife to his throat. "Where is she? What did you do?"

His mouth gaped like a fish. "You don't understand." Her knife bit into his throat, and he stilled. "Please. She made me do it."

"Made you do it." Just like Daddy said to Mama. "You think she made you do it?!" Delilah raised the knife high, then brought it down to pierce the center of his chest. "You monster!"

He gasped, and his face contorted. "Penny," he croaked.

"Don't you say my baby's name!" Delilah yanked the knife free and stabbed down again. "Don't you dare say her name!"

He gave a gurgling hiss, and blood bubbled from his mouth.

A scream—a voice she recognized as only a mother could—ripped Delilah's attention back toward the living room.

Sweet Pea.

Pea launched herself across the kitchen, shoving her mother off the man and dropping to her knees by his side. "Oh God! What did you do?" She looked up at Delilah, her face a mask of horror.

"You're alive." Delilah dropped the knife and reached out to touch her daughter, patting her back, squeezing her shoulder, stroking her hair. "Oh, baby, I was so scared."

Pea shoved Delilah, sending her sprawling, and pressed her hands to the man's chest. "You're going to be okay. Please, just hold on." Blood poured through her fingers.

Delilah watched, confusion fogging her mind.

"Sweet Pea?"

"Adam, wake up. Please, I need you." Pea gripped his face in her hands, pressed a kiss to his bloody lips. "Don't leave me."

Adam. Her daughter's boyfriend.

Tremors shook Delilah's body, gripped her muscles and shocked her bones.

Pea released Adam's face, and the boy's head lolled to the side to stare at Delilah. Not blinking. Not breathing.

Oh, God. What had she done?

Pea's shoulders slumped, and she turned to look up at her mother. Tears streamed down her cheeks. "You killed him."

Delilah swallowed, coughed, finally found her voice. "Charles was a monster. A monster. I thought he'd gotten you." She crawled closer to her daughter. "I thought he'd killed you."

"I knew what he was. That's swhy I went with him. He needed to be punished." Pea's laugh cut like jagged shards of glass.

"You knew?" Delilah's breath rushed in and out, in and out. "You saw?"

"The special tarts, your men, and before that, the knife. I watched you, learned from you." Pea dropped her chin to her chest; her hair curtained her face. "I wanted to prove to you I could help. That I could do what you do."

"No." Delilah never wanted this for her daughter, never wanted her to have this life. "No."

"Adam understood, you know? He accepted me." Pea stared down at her dead boyfriend. "What am I going to do?" Pea collapsed on Adam's body, muffled her sobs against his mangled chest.

Delilah's ribcage seemed to crack wide open, sending a lash of pain straight through her heart. "I didn't know. I thought he'd hurt you. I didn't know."

Delilah raised her hands up until they were all that she could see. Blood coated every inch of her skin from her fingertips to her wrists. The kind of blood that would never, ever wash away. The blood of an innocent.

"I'm so sorry," Delilah whispered. She'd hurt her Sweet Pea. Her baby.

Vision blurred with hot tears, Delilah felt along the floor until her fingers finally found the hilt of the knife.

"I…I didn't know you could see, too. I didn't know." How could she have been so stupid, so careless? All this time, her sweet baby had been watching her, learning from her. *Becoming* her. "I never wanted this life for you."

Pea looked up, her eyes widening at what she saw. She reached out toward her mother to stop her, but it was too late.

Delilah had been forced to take her daddy's life when he became a monster, but she refused to curse Pea with that same burden. "I love you," she said, and then sliced the blade across her own throat, hard and deep, and embraced the sharp pain she deserved.

IF HEARD, PLEASE CALL

I HEARD THE horn last week. It was so faint and distant I convinced myself it was my imagination, the resurfacing of a traumatic memory. But that horrible sound came back the next day and the next, louder and closer, just like last time. I'm terrified the train and the conductor who drives it are coming for me, for us. Again.

We lived on the edge of town back then. I guess we were poor, but I never noticed. Our house, a single-story with flaking white paint, sat at the outer edge of the neighborhood along a dirt road. The backyard bled into open field bisected by an abandoned set of rusted train tracks snaked with weeds.

My sister Rosey and I claimed the two bedrooms at the back of the house, the bigger one for me, as the big sister, and the smaller one for her. Lots of siblings fight, but not us. She was always small for her age and got sick a lot, so I made protecting her my personal mission. When we first moved into to town, and one of the boys from my second-grade class pushed her down and made her cry, I punched him right in the face and broke his nose. The little prick deserved it, and she worshiped me even more after that.

She always wanted a dog but couldn't have one because of her allergies, so I made sure she had the next best things. Whenever I saw a nice stuffed dog at Goodwill, I bought it for her with my allowance, or begged my parents until they caved. I bargained for a ratty Dog-Playing-Poker tapestry at a rummage sale and made our dad hang it in the hall that led to our rooms. We'd sit on the carpet in front of the picture, her stuffed animals at our sides, and play cards using our best dopey dog voices to say, "Go Fish" or "War."

That tapestry is in a box at the top of my closet now. I can't bear to look at it.

My room had a window that faced the field, and I arranged my bed against that wall. The brutal cold of the North Dakota winter would seep through the glass and insulated curtains, but I didn't mind. Lying there one night, cocooned in my blankets, is when I first heard the soft howl of the train's horn.

The next day I asked my parents about it, because I'd walked that open field and knew the tracks were over-grown and unused. They said the rail company hadn't transported through town in at least a decade, and that I probably dreamt the sound. But Rosey said she heard the horn, too. Over the next two weeks, we kept hearing the train getting louder and louder each night. Closer and closer. My parents laughed about it at first, then got angry with us, told us both to stop telling lies.

The night the train finally arrived was near the start of winter, when you aren't used to the cold yet and it seeps into your bones, threatens to crack them apart. The horn was so loud, I shuddered at the sound. Then, for the first time, I saw the bright glow of a headlight through the crack of my curtains. The light changed something, called to me like a lighthouse to a lost ship, and I couldn't resist that beacon.

I got out of bed, my body trembling with excitement. The weeks of waiting, of listening to the horn get closer, were finally over. The light and the barely perceptible rumble of the ground meant I hadn't imagined it. Clad only in long johns, socks, and a T-shirt, I stood on my bed and opened the window. Normally, the water-damaged wood casing resisted, but that night it slid up as if brand new. I went out feet first, stretched my toes until they reached the pile of cinder blocks my dad stacked behind the house. It was early October, and a thin layer of frost crusted the grass, stinging my feet through my socks. My breath misted in the air, but I didn't think for a minute about getting a coat or boots or gloves, all Dad's lectures about the dangers of frostbite forgotten. I only thought about reaching the train. It had finally come for me.

The moon was a bare crescent, and there were no streetlights that far out, but the headlight acted as a flare, drawing me into the field. I crept through the backyard, vaguely aware of shadowy figures stretching out beside and behind me. I wonder if I would have stopped, would have hesitated, if I had known one of them was Rosey.

The horn sounded again, wrapping my numb body in false warmth and drawing me forward. What felt like floating at the time was more likely a clumsy run, judging by the rips in the knees of my long johns, and the sharp rocks that had torn through my socks and embedded themselves in my feet—things which I discovered the following morning. As I crossed the field, anticipation fluttered in my throat like a swallowed moth thrashing about for freedom.

Pain sliced though my ankle and shattered my trance as I fell to the ground. My foot had gotten lodged in some animal's burrow. I yanked my leg free and tried to walk, but my broken ankle collapsed beneath me. Huddled on the ground, clutching my leg, I watched as the shadowy figures passed me, went on without me to the train tracks.

The light filled my vision and burned my eyes, as if I were staring at the sun, and the horn blew again, seeming to come from all directions and even from inside me. I screamed, maybe to answer it, maybe to release it, and I wasn't the only one. The others screamed, too, like a pack of ravenous wolves. We were at one with the horn, consumed by it and cracked wide open.

The next morning, I woke up to more screams, but not from kids this time, because I was the only one left alive. Someone gripped my body, lifted me from the ground with a Velcro-like tear that separated my frost-soaked clothes from the soil. The smell of motor oil and buttered popcorn blanketed me as my dad clutched me to his chest. Morning sun was shining through my eyelids, and I wanted to turn away, but I made myself look.

Thirty feet or so ahead of where I'd collapsed, body parts littered the ground along the train tracks, which were still snaked with weeds and unused. Blood trickled from still-open eyes and dribbled from disembodied ears. My mom cradled Rosey's body, mostly intact and clad in a flannel nightgown. One small foot was bruised and bare, and the other wore one of the Pound Puppy slippers I'd given her for her birthday. Rosey's head lolled to the side to look straight at me, accusing. I swiped at my face, and my fingers came away stained pink with blood and tears.

Twenty-three kids died that night, including my baby sister.

I struggled to remember what had happened that night, could only ever recall the horn and the light and the screams. Police officers, therapists, hypnotists, my parents—they all tried to pull something, anything, from my mind, but nothing ever worked.

We had to move soon after that. The others in the neighborhood wanted justice, and they resented me for not remembering. They'd hang around, wait for me to come outside, beg me for answers I couldn't give. My parents never held me responsible, but they also couldn't look at me the same, wouldn't ever make eye contact with me again.

It was my job to protect Rosey, and I failed. I bet if she had a dog, it wouldn't have forgotten her that night. It would've barked and blocked the window and refused to let her leave, no matter how bright that light was shining, or how loud that horn was blowing.

Now the train has come back for me, and maybe you, too. Do you hear it?

I made flyers to put up around my apartment building and the rest of the neighborhood—those kind with the tear-off phone numbers. The flyers say, "Do you hear the train getting closer? I do. Please call."

My neighbors think I'm crazy, I know. They avoid me, scurry past, take the stairs if I'm in the elevator. And yet, most of the tags with my phone number have been torn free from those flyers, so I know others hear it, too. They've probably even tried to call, but the conductor won't let us stop the train. Every time I pick up the ringing phone, there's only silence at first, then the soft howl of the horn. After the last time, I threw my phone out the window, smashed it onto the cement of the alley two stories below.

Yesterday, the horn was so loud it hurt my head to hear it, and my ankle began to throb. Today is the ten-year anniversary, exactly 3,652 days since that night. It's late and dark, and I know the light is coming for me. I nailed all my windows shut so I can't climb out, but I forgot the front door. I won't go, though, I know better this time, know that beacon is a lie.

Here comes the horn, so loud it rattles the dishes in my cupboards and threatens to pop my eardrums. I cover my ears, but the sound is now inside me. My feet burn with the sting of frost, and I'm thrust back to that night, to that frigid field swarming with ghosts.

A blazing light spills through the gap beneath the front door, from the hallway, and I hear her. Rosey is screaming. I stumble, but this time I don't fall. I don't break. Maybe it's not too late. Maybe I can still save her.

STARVED

MY MASS OF russet curls formed a barrier between me and the outside world, hiding my face and providing a veil of privacy. I scrawled in my journal, only stopping to pick at the black polish on my nails and flick the remnants to the vinyl floor. The flakes became fire ants that skittered up the pants legs of my classmates and sent them running through the hallowed halls of Red River High School, screaming.

Her perfume interrupted my fantasy, demanding attention. On the surface, a mix of vanilla and caramel. Underneath, a resinous bite. So sweet and sharp that I couldn't help but look up.

A girl I'd never seen before sat down at the desk in front of mine. She turned side-saddle in the chair and rested an elbow on my desk, propping her chin on one delicate hand. Perfectly bobbed black hair perfectly framed a face that was so beautiful it could belong to Aphrodite herself. The girl's eyes were as green as the purest jade, and I felt her gaze stealing my breath.

The untamed dragons of ancient myth had eyes like hers.

Her smile was just a hint, a mischievous twist of pale pink lips that ignited a flame I felt on every inch of my skin. "Want half?" she asked, holding out a foil-wrapped chocolate truffle.

I could only nod.

She peeled away the wrapper, extracted the pink sprinkle-topped chocolate, and neatly bit the piece in half. "Open," she said.

I did, and she placed the chocolate in my mouth. The flavor of rich dark-chocolate ganache and tangy raspberries melted on my tongue.

She licked her lips. "I'm Neve." Her voice was smoke in the air, husky and fleeting. "It means snow."

"Blindingly bright. Crystalline and liquid. Cold to the point of burning." The words spilled from my mouth, and I waited for her to laugh at me. Or worse, leave.

Her cheeks flushed, and she leaned closer until the entire world consisted of just her and me. "Don't keep me waiting, little poet. What's your name?"

A pool of warmth expanded inside my belly, molten and all-consuming. I took a deep, shaky breath, thoroughly affected. "Tessa."

She reached out and stroked her finger down my cheek, then tugged lightly on one of my rogue curls.

I had never been touched with that kind of affection, and the sensation left me dizzy.

"I might just have to keep you, little Tessa," she said.

I had never wanted anything so much in my whole life.

BEFORE NEVE, I was a ghost haunting a world that didn't want to see me. Born of blood and tragedy, the child of a monster, I was someone to be whispered about and avoided. Never touched. Never treasured.

She changed everything, made me want to come out of the shadows and into the light.

Neve consumed life like no one I'd ever known. Of course, she drew everyone to her, but she always made sure I had the spot right at her side, wedging me in at the lunch table, saving me a seat in class, making sure I rode shotgun anywhere we went.

I basked in the melody of her voice, the tickle of her laughter, and most of all the ecstasy with which she ate. Food had always been necessary to me, nothing more. Neve taught me that eating was a singular pleasure, a communing of the senses.

Whether we were at school, in a restaurant, or in her bedroom, she watched each time I tried a new bite, a new flavor. Curries and pastas and buttered popcorn and milkshakes. A poetry of tastes that she wanted to share with me alone.

I heard what people said, that Neve was so very generous, so caring to befriend the little abused whelp abandoned even by her drunkard father. But none of them understood.

I loved Neve, and she loved me. I was hers, and she was mine.

After our first—and my very first—kiss, Neve whispered, "This is our secret."

She'd pulled me into the empty girls' bathroom and shut us inside a stall so that we were pressed close. The touch of her lips had left my heart fluttering in my chest like a newly hatched butterfly emerging from its cocoon. "Something for only us two."

"Yes, my little Tessa." Her breath tickled the shell of my ear. "You always understand."

I lived for our stolen moments, for her secret smiles, for the light touches that told me I was hers. When we were apart, I fed on my memories of her. My journals were filled with sonnets for her, with odes to her, with the sketched likeness of her face. Even in sleep, I dreamed only of her.

We were so perfectly happy, and I knew I would never ever be alone in the dark again.

FOR MONTHS, SHE was mine alone. Then *he* came. I knew him, everyone did. He played on the rugby team and insisted on wearing his uniform to class on game days. Sauntering through the halls, his voice dominated every conversation and assaulted my ears as he performed for his acolytes.

He managed to wedge himself into my normal spot at the long cafeteria table during lunch, right beside Neve, between her and me. But I couldn't stop him, not without making a scene. Others sat around us, drawn by her, as always, but their words only buzzed in the background like teeming insects.

I watched as she talked to him, as she laughed with him, as she touched his hand, his arm.

As she fed him a piece of soft brie on bread, leaving nothing for me.

Clutching my hands in my lap beneath the table, twisting them almost hard enough to break my own fingers like dry twigs, I told myself it was just one time, that nothing had changed.

After school, we were blessedly alone again. I wanted to take her hand as we approached the parking lot, but knew I'd have to wait until we were enclosed in the stale, delicious heat of her car. There, she would be mine again.

But she stopped, looked back toward the sports fields, a collection of bleachers and goal posts and bright lights and excited cheers that made me want to flee to the shadows.

"There's a game tonight, rugby. Want to go?"

The question sucked the air from my lungs. She wanted to see *him*.

"Come on. Let's go watch those brutes bash each other. It'll be fun."

"I prefer a kiss to such violence," I said, though I knew we would do whatever she liked. However much it hurt, any pain with her was better than the pain of being without her.

She pulled me back toward the school, led me to a spot hidden from view between a tall hedge and the rough brown brick of the building, and laced her fingers with mine. "You can't just hide away, little Tessa. There is a real world out there that is aching and beautiful."

Her touch was a salve, a reminder that she did love me, that she wanted to share things with me. So, we went to the game. We sat on hard metal bleachers and cheered as we watched the boys fight over a ball. We ate warm peanuts, and gooey nachos, and hot dogs with relish from paper boats, licking our fingers clean.

And she was right. There was a beauty to the brutality, like a macabre ballet. It left me breathless and thankful. She was always pushing me, always showing me new and wonderful things. Making me want to come out into the light.

But after the match, she insisted we say hello to the boy, now smeared with filth from the game. We caught him at the corner of the empty field, away from the other players and fans. Feeling exposed, I hung back behind Neve, wishing the wind would stop carrying his stink to my nose.

She spoke to him, and she touched him again, wiping away a drip of blood from the corner of his lip and sucking it off the tip of her finger.

My stomach curdled at the site of her tasting him so intimately.

"A bunch of us are going over to the Pizza Palace. You guys should come." He shoved one hand through his sweat-dampened hair and leered at her. I knew he wanted her for his own.

But she was mine.

I grabbed her wrist, unable to stop myself, and let the poetry in my heart speak. "But we eat with eyes and ears, consuming light and words and whispers."

She glared at me, tugged free of my grasp.

"Yeah, I think I'd rather *consume* pizza," he said, watching me like I was some alien species behind glass.

Neve laughed, and it wasn't the husky laugh that sent shivers over my skin. This was sandpaper, grating me raw with its cruelty. "Pizza sounds great. I've got my dad's car if you want a ride."

He forgot about me, wholly focused on her now.

"I'd love a ride."

"Tessa's not hungry, are you?" Her dragon's eyes cut me like a razor's edge.

"No, I..." I wondered if I'd ever be hungry again.

Neve nodded. That was the answer she wanted. "See you tomorrow, 'kay?"

And she left me there.

"Later, Trisha," the boy said, following after her and throwing his arm possessively across her shoulders.

"Tessa," I said to myself as my stomach turned and bile rose up to sting my throat. I watched them walk away. Touching. Laughing. Soon they would be eating. Spicy pepperoni. Stringy melted cheese. Rich marinara.

Would she devour him, as she had devoured me?

I bent over and vomited in the dying grass.

I CREPT THROUGH the rose bushes toward Neve's bedroom window, feeling the tug of thorns on my T-shirt, as if they were trying to keep me from her. I tapped on the glass.

The heavy curtains swayed, and she peeked through the gap, her eyes rounding with surprise, then narrowing.

"Please." I needed a chance to show her, to explain. "Can we talk?"

She opened the window, and relief swept through my veins. The room was lit only by candles, a soft flicker against the aubergine walls.

I boosted myself up on the electrical box, the movement a muscle memory from so many repetitions, and entered the room where we'd shared everything, the room that was more a home to me than any other place ever had been. The plush gray carpet that tickled bare feet, the white vanity where she'd pampered my skin and hair, making me feel beautiful for the first time, the TV that played black-and-white movies late into the night as we snuggled beneath the heavy velvet comforter blanketing her bed. It was my paradise.

She didn't draw me into her arms though, not that night, and I knew things weren't fixed yet. But they would be.

She plopped down at the vanity, facing away from me. A small cutting board sat atop the surface, and she continued her work of slicing a crisp green apple into wedges. "What are you doing here, Tessa?"

I wanted to sit with her on the bed, caress her skin, thread my fingers through her raven hair. "You draw me to you like a flame—"

She slammed down the knife, and the vanity's mirror swayed, warping the reflection of my face. "Just talk like a normal person."

I cringed. Normal, something I had never been. "I had to see you."

"We shouldn't. Not anymore." She raised a slice of apple to her perfect lips. I wished she'd extend her hand and offer me a bite, let me experience the sweet-and-sour taste of the apple's flesh with her.

"We can go back to the way things were," I said, moving closer.

"Why?"

"We're meant to be together. Forever."

"Is that what you really think?"

"I'm the one you need." I took another step and reached out to her.

She cringed, as if the thought of my touch disgusted her. "We had some fun, yeah, but that's all it was."

"That boy. He can't make you happy, not like I can."

She sighed. "This has nothing to do with him."

"He's poisoned you, hasn't he?" My arm dropped to my side. I never should have let her go with him. I should have protected her.

"You're not listening. We're through. Understand?"

Her words snatched my breath, and my knees threatened to buckle. "No. You love me."

She stood, her hands fisted at her sides. "I never said I loved you."

The hammering of my pulse filled my ears like the crash of ocean waves. "I can't live without you."

"Stop being so fucking dramatic." She turned her back to me and started toward the bedroom door. "And don't come back here again."

I rushed around her, blocking her path. "You can't leave me."

"Get out of my way."

"You remember the heat of my skin." I grasped her arms in a tight grip, holding her there. I had to make her understand.

Her emerald eyes flashed, and she slapped me, her hand searing my skin.

Shocked, I let her go, raising my hand to my cheek to feel the exquisite imprint of her touch. Pain split my lip and I trailed my finger along it, collecting a dribble of blood. My breath stuttering, I took my finger into my mouth and let the coppery essence coat my tongue.

She gaped at me, frozen.

Licking the blood from my lips, I reached for her again. "I love you."

"Stop." She backed away, looking from side to side. Her gaze landed on the butcher knife on the vanity, and her face twisted into something ugly and angry. She snatched up the knife, brandishing it at *me.*

That boy's poison was taking hold of her. "You won't hurt me."

She swiped the blade through the air between us. "Just get out of here. Get away from me."

"I know you, truly." I lunged toward her, wrapping my hands around the hilt of the knife over top of hers. "And you know me. Look closely. See me."

I yanked her toward me, bringing the knife point just beneath my chin.

"You're crazy." She bared her teeth and jerked the blade back toward her, pulling too hard.

I let go, couldn't hold on, and the gleaming, silver blade pierced the smooth, pale skin of her neck.

"No," I whispered. "No."

She gasped, her lips and chin trembling, and dropped the knife.

A spray of arterial blood gushed from the wound, drenching my hands, my face, my neck, my chest.

She wilted to the floor, and I fell to my knees beside her.

"Help … me." She gaped up at me, like a fish drowning on air, as she clutched at her throat.

I pressed my hands over the top of hers, but blood pumped through our fingers. She stared up at me, the shimmering green of her eyes eaten away by the black of her pupils.

Neve gave a choking cough that turned her lips scarlet and sprayed my face with a warm splatter, then her hands went limp beneath mine, and her head lolled to the side.

"You can't leave me. I'll starve without you. I'll starve." The coppery tinge of her blood dripped into my mouth and coated my tongue, mingling with my own salty tears.

It was a flavor like nothing she had ever shown me before. Intense. Heartbreaking. Delicious. The taste of life and despair, of love and pain.

I knew how to save her, how to keep her alive. She'd taught me, she'd shown me in preparation for this very moment. I knew how to keep her forever.

Leaning over her, I placed a soft kiss on her lips. They seemed to move beneath mine, telling me that, yes, this was the way for us to be together. I licked at her mouth, lapping up the coppery essence of her life, but there wasn't enough.

More, I needed more of her. I needed everything. I hunched over her neck, over the gash that had once sprayed and now just wept. And I tasted her and loved her and let her fill me up in a beautiful communion.

"I LOVE YOU, my little Tessa," Neve whispered, her breath tickling my ear, raising the hairs on my neck.

I never tired of hearing those words. "You're my everything, my life," I said, rolling on my side, the white floor a soft cushion beneath my body, a gigantic bed.

"Who're you talking to, Tessa?" the man, one of the doctors, asked. He sat in a folding chair he would take with him when he left, a clipboard balanced on his lap.

A mischievous smile tugged at my lips.

"He doesn't understand," Neve said in a husky voice only I could hear.

I giggled. "No one does. It's something for only us two."

"Yes, our secret," she said.

The man left. I knew there would be more, always talking, always asking, always writing on their clipboards, never understanding.

I rolled onto my back and opened my eyes, letting the whiteness of the room fill my vision.

Sometimes they put me in the place with the twin bed and the flowered wallpaper and the barred window. Twice they brought me to a big room with tables and chairs and games and people. That place made me angry, too loud and busy and crowded, distracting me from my Neve. I screamed and hit them and hit myself until they brought me back to the white room.

That is where I saw her best, where she came to life on the blank canvas of the walls. That is where I heard her most clearly, the quiet stillness an echo chamber for her voice. I bit my lip and the taste of our blood, coppery and rich as that first chocolate, bloomed on my tongue and left me hungry for her. She was inside me, and she loved me always, knowing that I saved her, that I devoured her as she did me so we would be together forever.

RETURN OF THE WILDERNESS GIRLS

I OPENED MY eyes to tiny, muted pinpricks of light. Stars in a dark, moonless sky. Water soaked my clothes, sending shivers over my skin, and I struggled to my feet, knew I should run. Branches reached out with spindly fingers to tear at my arms and snag my hair. Tree roots surged to catch my bare toes, sending me sprawling on the ground again and again.

The barking of a dog ripped through the silence, and a brilliant white light blazed, illuminating a path through the woods. I followed the beacon, bursting through the trees to fall down on the pavement.

Figures emerged from the shadows to surround me. A tall man in a brimmed hat crouched, his badge glinting in the light.

"Can you stand?" he asked. His weathered face sagged with wrinkles, like he'd shrunk inside his skin.

I swallowed and tried to talk, but no words came. I nodded.

He took my elbow to help me up.

I surveyed the rest of the group, more officers, then looked down at myself. A sopping-wet cotton nightgown that had been white at some point stuck to my skin, and my long brown hair hung clumped and matted over my shoulder. Scratches marred my bare arms and legs, but I didn't feel any pain.

I didn't feel anything.

The officer wrapped a blanket around my shoulders. "My name is Sheriff Jeffries. I'm going to help you."

He steered me toward the caged backseat of the police car, and I tried to pull away, but he tightened his hold. "It's all right. Just a short ride to town."

Shaking, I let him lead me to the rear passenger door. The rest of the officers followed us, watching me as the sheriff reached across to buckle my seat belt.

"Where are you taking me?"

"Your mom has been waiting for you for a very long time."

My mom. I searched my memories, but there was nothing. I winced at the pain that spiked through my skull.

"Don't try too hard to remember." He pushed up the brim of his hat. "That's when it hurts."

"How did you know?"

"It's the same for all the girls." He closed the door, shutting me inside.

"Yes," I whispered, knowing there were others.

THE CRUISER'S HEADLIGHTS cut through the darkness of the winding mountain road. I stared straight ahead, refusing to look into the woods that pressed in on us from either side, and tucked my legs up under the blanket.

"Are you cold?" The sheriff eyed me in the rearview mirror and reached for the knob to turn up the heat.

"How long until we reach town?" Would the other girls be waiting for me? I hoped so. The need to see them pressed against my chest until I could hardly breathe.

"About five minutes." He cleared his throat. "You're probably wondering why you were in those woods."

"Huh." I should care how I got there, but since hearing about the others, I'd thought of nothing else. "I guess."

"We're not really sure. You girls started returning about a year ago, one on every new moon."

"Thirteen. There are thirteen of us." I knew I was the last.

His knuckles whitened on the steering wheel. "Never have understood how you do that. Don't know your own names, but you remember each other."

"Not remember. I just know." I rubbed my hands over my arms, the blanket not enough to warm me. How could I know about the girls, but recall nothing of myself? "What is my name?"

"Roberta."

"Roberta." I tried it out, wanting to feel something, but it was just a word. "You said I have a mother."

"She's going to be mighty glad to see you." He sighed. "Most of us mourned you girls years ago, but Colleen, she never gave up hope you'd come back."

"Years." I wondered how many, started to ask, when the trees thinned and peeled away from the road. Streetlights dotted either side and illuminated crumbling shops with faded paint, broken windows, and dangling shingles.

People of all ages lined the sidewalks, most dressed in pajamas as if they'd been pulled from their beds and lined along the street like props. They glared at the sheriff's car, at me, as we rolled past.

"Don't worry about them. They're just scared. A thing like this, well, it's hard to understand."

I unclipped my seatbelt and turned to peer out the back window at the people still watching me.

He pulled the car up in front of a brick building. The sign above the door said Black Lake Sheriff's Department.

I pointed to the only words that seemed familiar. "Black Lake."

"We thought about renaming the town after what happened but never did." He shrugged and opened his door. "You ready?"

"Yes." I hoped the girls were inside waiting.

He rounded the car to open my door, and I stepped onto the curb, the cement rough against my bare feet. The townspeople poured down the sidewalk and into the road, advancing toward me. I shrunk back against the car, and the blanket slipped from my shoulders.

"Go on home, folks. Roberta here needs some space." The sheriff stood in front of me.

"That girl ain't right," a voice called from the crowd, earning shouts of agreement.

I flinched. What had I done to earn the hatred of these people?

The sheriff rested his hand on the butt of his gun. "Go on home. Now."

Grumbles of protest passed through the crowd, but they disbursed, many craning their necks to glower at me as they walked away.

He picked up the blanket, wrapped it back around my shoulders, and led me toward the station. I ignored the urge to look back, focusing instead on the prospect of seeing the others as I stepped across the threshold and through the door to the station.

A half wall closed off most of the room. Four empty desks sat on the opposite side of the wall, and behind them a door opened. A woman wearing a blue, knee-length dress ran out, giving a strangled cry at the sight of me. Her face was thin and pale, all eyes and mouth surrounded by a cloud of curly brown hair.

"My baby." She stumbled through the room on high heels, banging into a chair as she passed the desks. The sheriff opened the waist-high door set in the half wall, allowing the woman to hurtle toward me. "I knew you'd come home."

I tensed as she wrapped her arms around me and buried her face in my neck. The urge to push her away was almost overpowering, but I resisted, fisting my hands at my sides.

A woman in a floral dress came toward us, with the assistance of a metal cane. The graying bun perched on her head wobbled with each step. "Colleen, remember what we talked about?" She patted my mother's shoulder. "This is all very overwhelming for her."

"Oh, yes. Right." My mother released her hold, and I took a step back.

She swiped at her cheeks, then smoothed the front of her dress with both hands. "Roberta, I'm your momma. You remember me, don't ya?" Desperate hope oozed from her pores, threatening to choke me.

The sheriff shared a look with the other lady and stepped up beside my mother. "She's got amnesia like the rest."

My mother frowned. "Of course, I know. I just hoped—"

"The other girls." I clutched his sleeve. "Are they here?"

The other woman sidled closer. "I'm Mrs. Shepherd. We're so happy to have you back, Roberta." She looked me up and down, her eyes catching on each scrape, each bruise. "I run a home for the girls called Angel House. They're anxious to meet you."

"Now? Are you taking me there?"

My mother pushed past Mrs. Shepherd. "I'm taking you home with me. I've got everything ready. Your room is just like you left it."

I opened my mouth, ready to say no, I don't want to go with you.

"We have a paramedic on the way to check you out. After that, you'll go with your mom." The sheriff's eyes met mine in a silent plea. "She needs you with her now."

"You'll see the other girls tomorrow. I promise," Mrs. Shepherd said.

THE HOUSE WAS small and worn, with a cracked concrete path leading from the sidewalk to a set of wooden stairs that creaked beneath my feet.

My mother rushed ahead of me to open the door and flip on the lights.

I stepped over the threshold. Photos lined the wall, and I studied the pictures of a perfect little family frozen in time, reaching out to brush my fingers across the face of the young girl with the too-big smile.

"You were always so happy," my mother said.

I didn't recognize myself, and pain sliced through my head at the attempt to recall even the smallest pieces of my life. Moving down the line of pictures, I took in the family photos, the candid vacation shots, the birthdays. When I reached the picture of a group of girls in matching shorts and vests, I stopped.

"The girls." I didn't recognize their faces, but I knew it was them.

"I knew the Wilderness Girls was too dangerous, but your father insisted, always had to have his way." Venom coated her words.

"Is he here?"

She turned away. "He passed last year. Liver failure."

I cocked my head to the side. My father was dead. Should I feel sad?

"Let me fix you something to eat. You must be hungry." She continued down the hall.

I followed her, examining the place that used to be my home. The living room to the right held a ragged green couch facing a television. More photos dotted the walls, a shrine to the young girl—me. A "Welcome Home" banner hung draped above the television, and streamers crisscrossed the ceiling.

My throat tightened under some invisible pressure.

I shuffled into the kitchen, where my mother flitted from the fridge to the tattered cupboards, gathering supplies. She placed a pan on the stove and turned on the heat, then tore the plastic from a package of hamburger and set it beside her on the counter.

The smell of meat drew me into the room.

"Mrs. Shepherd told me about your diet, about what you'd need when you returned." My mother dropped a patty into the pan. "She said raw was best, but I know my baby. You always liked them well done."

Saliva flooded my mouth. I snatched the package of meat from the counter and slid into a chair at the table in the corner, indifferent to the scratch of the cracked upholstery on the backs of my thighs. I grabbed a handful of hamburger and took a bite, the coppery flavor blooming on my tongue.

My mother gasped, one hand covering her mouth. "I, uh, guess you were pretty hungry."

I took another bite of hamburger, paying no attention to the blood that seeped through my fingers to drip down my arms.

"IT'S EXACTLY HOW you left it." My mother watched me from the doorway. "I haven't touched a thing."

I stood in the center of the pink carpet, waiting for something to look familiar. A white wood-framed bed with a comforter to match the carpet sat against one wall, and a white desk was positioned beneath the room's only window. Framed tracings of leaves hung on the walls, along with insects and butterflies pinned behind glass. My headache grew, pulsing against my skull.

She pulled open a dresser drawer. "After the first girl came back, I picked up some clothes. I kept praying the next one would be you."

I peered into the drawer at the clothes in shades of pink and purple that still held price tags.

"The bathroom is down the hall. I'm sure you want to clean up. There's a fresh towel for you, and I got your favorite strawberry shampoo."

"Okay." Her nervousness crawled across my skin like an electric shock, and I gripped the doorknob, willing her to leave.

"I've missed you so much, Roberta." She reached out to touch me, but I leaned away. Her hands fluttered in the air like wounded birds, until she clasped them together as if in prayer. "I'll take care of you, give you whatever you want."

My stomach twisted at the neediness in her voice. She was just trying to show her daughter she cared. "Thank you."

"The other girls…" She licked her lips. "They didn't have enough support at home, but that won't happen here. You'll want to stay with me."

I rubbed my hands on the dirty cotton of my nightgown. "I'm tired."

"Of course." Her eyes filled with moisture. "We'll talk more tomorrow."

She backed into the hall, and I started to close the door. "I love you," she said, just before the latch clicked shut.

My shoulders hunched. I clenched my eyes closed and pictured her face, trying to recall anything about her or my father. Agony sliced through my head, sending lights bursting behind my eyes.

I took several deep breaths, and the pain faded. Slumping onto the bed, I picked up one of the stuffed animals piled against the pillow, a white bear. I brushed my thumb through the fur of his cheek, leaving a streak of dirt on his face.

The air charged, making the hair on my arms stand straight up, and I knew they'd come. I left the bear behind and crossed to the window to pull back the curtains.

The girls.

All twelve of them stood in the street. They varied in height, hair color, and skin tone, but shared the same thin frame and focused expression. I didn't recognize a single one, but I knew them all.

I pressed my palm to the cool glass.

They reached up, extending their arms toward me. Soon, we'd all be together.

Movement on the front porch caught my eye. My mother rushed down the steps. "Go home. She doesn't need you. Go away."

They lowered their arms but didn't move.

She followed their gaze to my window, to my hand still pressed to the glass, and her face drained of color.

MY MOTHER DIDN'T say much at breakfast the next morning, just placed some raw meat on a plate and gave it to me with the request that I use a fork. She'd abandoned her church-ready outfit from the night before, opting for threadbare sweatpants and a brown sweater that she wrapped around herself like a cocoon.

"I need to see the girls." My words rang through the silence of the house.

Her lip trembled. "Don't you like it here?"

I wiped my mouth, smearing the napkin red, and tried to figure out how to explain.

She lowered her chin to her chest. "I'd hoped you'd be different, that you might need me."

"I know." My stomach turned with guilt that I couldn't be the daughter she wanted.

She grabbed my plate and stood by the sink with her back to me. "Go pack, then. I'll drive you."

Something in her voice caused a tearing in my chest, but it was nothing compared to the ache I felt being apart from the girls. I retreated to the bedroom to shove some clothes into a bag, my pulse racing at the knowledge we'd soon be reunited.

When I returned to the living room, I found my mother sitting on the couch, her eyes fixed on the trashed banner and streamers piled in the center of the room. She'd finally realized her daughter was never coming home.

As we drove across town, I pretended not to notice the tears dripping down her cheeks. We rounded a corner and Angel House came into view, a charcoal-gray Victorian with black trim and shutters, perched on a hill that overlooked the rest of the neighborhood.

She parked the car, then got out to retrieve my bag from the trunk.

I stood on the sidewalk, staring up at the house. The girls were inside. I could feel them. My mother came to stand beside me, placing the bag at my feet.

A twinge of regret needled though me. "I'm sure your daughter loved you very much."

She wrapped her arms around her middle, as if trying to keep herself from splitting apart.

"I'm sorry." I picked up the bag and slung it over my shoulder, then rushed up the stairs to Angel House.

The front door swung open to reveal Mrs. Shepherd, wearing another floral print dress. She glanced behind me at my mother and gave a sad smile. "Come in, dear."

A prickle of awareness washed over my skin as I stepped inside, and the bag slipped from my shoulder. I continued through an arched doorway into the living room, where the girls stood.

One girl, the first, stepped forward while the rest converged to surround me in a loose circle. "We've been waiting for you." She reached out to touch my cheek.

The rest of the girls placed their hands on my arms, my shoulders, my back. A tension I didn't know I'd been carrying seeped from my muscles.

"Alright now, girls, let's give Roberta some space." Mrs. Shepherd rapped her cane against the floor, and the girls stepped back as a group. "Adelaide, would you take the others and prepare lunch, please?"

The first girl inclined her head, then turned and exited through another doorway on the adjacent wall. The rest of the girls followed, like a flock of birds moving in unison. As if pulled on a string, I stepped after them.

Mrs. Shepherd grabbed my wrist. "Chat with me a minute, dear." She tugged me over to the sofa, upholstered in another of the floral prints she seemed so fond of, and took a seat.

I perched on the edge, my eyes straying to the doorway the girls had gone through.

"You'll be staying with us from now on then, will you?" She rested her hands in her lap.

"Yes." No temptation struck me to return to the place I once called home, to the woman I once called mother.

"Do you remember anything?"

I shook my head. "No. What happened to us?"

"When I was a child, my grandfather spun tales of the Black Lake, warning us of the evil that lurked there." She gazed out the front window that dominated the wall behind the sofa. "Just as each of us has a darkness that resides within, whispering in our ears, this town has the Black Lake."

My mouth went dry, and I swallowed to soothe my parched throat.

"I don't know what possessed Patty, your troop leader, to take you girls camping in those woods at all, much less on the dark night of the new moon." She pulled back the sheer drapes covering the window and tapped on the glass.

I craned my neck to peek through the curtains. A murder of crows dotted the barren branches of the oak tree that dominated the front yard.

She let the drapes fall back into place. "Patty woke in the night to find the tents empty and you girls gone. Driven by some deep instinct, she ran for the lake and found only flashlights, shoes, and jackets abandoned on the shore."

I struggled to take a full breath. We'd all just jumped into the lake and disappeared? There had to be more to it than that.

"Did you hear the whispers as you lay in your sleeping bags, I wonder?" Mrs. Shepherd said, almost to herself. She met my gaze. "We dredged the lake and searched the woods, but you'd all vanished. That was five years ago."

I rubbed my hands up and down my arms. "Where could we have been all that time?"

"Only you girls and the Black Lake can answer that question, dear."

UNDER THE GUIDANCE of Adelaide and the others, I fell into the rhythm of Angel House. In the mornings, we'd prepare a meal of raw meat, and after breakfast, several teachers visited to tutor us.

They attempted to enroll Adelaide in school after she returned, but there had been an incident. A boy got too friendly, and she bit him. The board decided she didn't belong with the others our age, that she was dangerous. When the next girl attacked her parents, Mrs. Shepherd offered to take them both in. That was the start of Angel House.

After morning lessons, we ate lunch and did chores. The rest of the afternoon was free time. We could spend it reading, lounging in the garden, or watching television. Whatever the diversion, the girls always chose the same thing, none of us having any desire to part from the group. I stopped trying to remember my life before and focused on this new life with the girls. They calmed me.

One fascination we all shared was the moon. The cycles, the phases, the rotation. The coming of the next new moon became a beacon in our minds, and an internal clock ticked down to that day. Previously, the occurrence had marked the arrival of a new girl, but I was the last.

By the week before the new moon, we became increasingly agitated. Unable to sleep through the night, we drifted through Angel House like restless ghosts, only finding peace when we sat in the frost-covered grass and stared up at the starry sky.

We became hungrier, too. The craving for meat, for flesh, was a constant companion, an empty ache in my stomach that refused to be sated.

Sheriff Jeffries paid us a visit, alerted by Mrs. Shepherd to the changes in our behavior. He wanted to know if anything else would happen, if the town should be worried. We couldn't answer, because we didn't know.

Maybe I should have been afraid of what was coming, but I didn't come back with the ability to feel fear. Like many of the most primitive creatures, I simply lived each day driven by the demands of my physical body, my mind, and my instincts.

The day before the new moon, Mrs. Shepherd decided we should get out of the house and go into town. Adelaide agreed. We all agreed.

We ambled down main street, with Mrs. Shepherd in the lead, as signs flipped behind shop windows to "Closed" and tattered blinds were pulled to block the interior from our eyes. We weren't welcome. My memory flashed back to the people lining the street the night of my return, glaring at the police car. If anything, their hatred of us had festered and grown stronger.

Mrs. Shepherd approached a jewelry store and someone inside flipped the lock closed as her hand touched the knob. She turned to face us with a huff, pasting a smile on her face. "Don't you worry, girls. Some folks get scared of things they don't understand. They'll come around." She angled her chin toward her van parked at the end of the block. "Let's head on home. We'll swing by the grocery store and pick up steaks for dinner."

She hobbled along on her cane, and we followed. I couldn't help but peer into the storefronts as we passed, watching my own reflection, that of a harmless girl. What did the townspeople see that I didn't?

Up the street, a door banged open, and a man stumbled out of a business called "Old Tom's Bar" still holding a beer bottle. He wore grimy jeans and a flannel shirt that strained against his belly. "I been waiting for you girls to show your faces." He sneered and took an unsteady step toward us.

Mrs. Shepherd jabbed her cane toward him. "You stop right there, George Kennedy. We don't need any trouble."

I moved closer to the girl next to me, and she did the same, until all of us huddled in a tight group.

He pointed at us, his hand trembling. "My Patty is dead because of them girls." Tears leaked from his eyes. He swiped the back of his hand across his face, sloshing beer on his shirt.

Mrs. Shepherd backed up. "These girls didn't lay a finger on her."

What did this man think we'd done?

"My Patty was happy. If they'd have stayed in their goddamn tents, she wouldn't have done what she did. She never would've left me."

Along the street, shop owners crept from their stores to watch.

Mrs. Shepherd glanced at us over her shoulder. "You girls go wait for me at the car."

Adelaide hesitated for a moment, then did as instructed, leading us back the way we came. Just like that first night, the people outside the shops glared as we passed. Their faces were foreign to me, strangers. Except one. My breath caught in my throat when I realized who it was. My mother. She waved a silent hello.

I started to raise my hand in reply, when her eyes widened, and she sprung toward me.

Pain exploded across the back of my skull, and I fell to my knees. I pressed my fingers to the back of my head. They came away coated red. The girls cried out all around me, as if they, too, had been struck.

"Someone call 9-1-1." My mother broke through the girls to kneel beside me.

My pulse rushed through my ears as I stared at the brown glass shards littering the ground beside me. The long, thin neck of the beer bottle remained intact.

I pushed my mother away and stood, spinning to face George. The girls moved with me.

"No. I didn't mean…" He turned in a circle, his gaze jumping from person to person. He pushed past Mrs. Shepherd and staggered toward us.

"Don't you lay a hand on those girls!" Mrs. Shepherd yelled, her face red as she hobbled after him. "Someone stop him! Help us!"

No one moved.

George collapsed at my feet and began scraping the glass up with his bare hands, leaving a trail of blood on the sidewalk.

The sharp, coppery aroma stung my nose, fresh and vibrant, and dark hunger twisted my stomach. The girls shifted in tighter behind me. They smelled it, too. My craving for flesh overwhelmed everything else, consuming me, and I pounced on him, pushing him to the ground as the girls closed in around me.

I tore his shirt aside to expose his shoulder. He thrashed beneath me, but I held on tight. I bit down hard, teeth piercing skin and muscle, then shook my head to tear a delicious piece of flesh free. His horrified shrieks split the air and multiplied as they spread through the crowd. I chewed and swallowed as the girls ripped at his clothes, eager to taste.

Hands grasped me from behind, pulled me away. No. I needed more of the meat, I had to have it. I growled and tried to lunge back on top of him, but the hands were too many and too strong. Most of the other girls' teeth found bare skin before they, too, were pulled away, blood staining their faces and flesh hanging from their mouths.

Police officers and townspeople swarmed us, holding the girls back as George screamed and screamed.

SHERIFF JEFFRIES PACED the living room of Angel House, stopping to peer out the front window at the townspeople gathered on the sidewalk.

We'd been released from jail earlier in the day, pending criminal charges. The crowd started to gather outside after we arrived home and steadily grew in size as night fell, people of all ages joining the group to shout insults and demand justice.

They said we were evil, called us demons. But we weren't demons, were we? The hunger was just so powerful, impossible to resist once blood spilled. I knew I should feel guilty for my behavior, but I didn't. Denying my desire for flesh would be like a tiger resisting the need to hunt and kill its prey.

"The State Police are coming to transport you to a safer location. We just have to hold out a few hours." The sheriff rubbed one hand over his face.

Mrs. Shepherd tried to send us to bed, but none of us could sleep with the constant barrage of shouts from the crowd. We'd crept from our beds and stood huddled together in the center of the room, clothed in matching white nightgowns.

"Where will they take us?" Adelaide asked.

"A juvenile facility upstate," he said.

Mrs. Shepherd moved toward us, then stopped. She hadn't dared get close since the incident. "They're better equipped to handle you girls, at least until we can figure out how to treat…whatever is happening to you." She was convinced we were plagued by some mysterious sickness and needed only to be cured.

"Will we be able to stay together?" I couldn't stand the thought of being separated.

"I don't know, dear." Mrs. Shepherd stared at the carpet, not meeting our eyes.

Something crashed through the window, tearing the drapes and littering the sofa with broken glass. A rock. The screams of the gathering mob rose, and the sheriff rushed out the front door with his weapon drawn. His voice carried over the chants of the crowd. "Everyone needs to leave. Additional officers are en route, and we will take you into custody if you remain on this property."

A scuffle sounded on the front porch, and Mrs. Shepherd limped into the entry hallway.

Gunshots sounded, and Sheriff Jeffries cried out.

I clutched the hand of the girl beside me.

The front door slammed open, and Mrs. Shepherd was shoved back into the wall. Several men holding shotguns pushed past her and entered the living room. Their faces all shared the same crazed expression, eyes bulging and mouths contorted. One of them raised his weapon level with my face.

Adelaide stepped from the group of girls as one of the men moved forward, his gun held at his side. "Father?"

The man's face flushed, and his finger twitched on the trigger. "You are not my daughter, demon."

I stared into the black void of the double barrel shotgun, imagining the pellets ripping through my skin. "Why are you doing this?" These people had once loved us as daughters, friends, and neighbors.

Adelaide's father turned his attention to me. "We were fooled into thinking the girls we lost came back to us, but you are nothing but vessels of the devil. We're taking you back where you came from."

Mrs. Shepherd tried to elbow her way past the other men. "You've already shed innocent blood tonight. Stop this now, before it's too late."

Adelaide held up her hand. "It's okay, we'll go."

"No." Mrs. Shepherd fisted her hands in the collar of her dress. "They have no right to do this."

"You've been kind to us, but it's time we left. We don't belong here." Adelaide strode toward the front door, and the girls followed.

Though we were handing ourselves over to the mob, I wasn't frightened. Everything would be okay as long as we were together.

Adelaide's father grabbed her by the upper arm, stopping on the top step of the porch to brandish his prize. "Tonight, righteousness will prevail. We will cast out these devils and send them back to hell."

The crowd cheered and continued to spit insults as we trailed Adelaide down the steps. I looked back at Mrs. Shepherd struggling against the man who held her back. "There is nothing righteous in harming these girls! God will judge all of you this night!" she yelled.

BAREFOOT AND CLOTHED only in a cotton nightgown, I shivered from the cold air and frigid asphalt. We were herded down main street, surrounded by the shouting mob. People lined the sidewalks to watch, but none of them intervened.

I glimpsed my mother's face in the crowd. She didn't wave this time.

As we walked, we were shoved to the ground, then kicked until we got up again. The spectators pelted us with rocks and rushed into the street to hit us or pull out chunks of our hair. Pain throbbed through my head, my stomach, and my knee. Blood filled my mouth. The faces of our tormentors warped in my mind, twisting into feral things, beasts hidden in human form.

We passed the edge of town and continued down the dark mountain road. The townspeople's flashlights bobbed in the darkness, illuminating the trees towering on either side.

My pounding heart calmed as we progressed farther along the road, and the agitation that had been beating against my skin abated as the new moon approached. The cold turned me numb, and my pain ebbed, becoming nothing more than the buzzing of an insect in the back of my mind.

The Black Lake called to us like a beacon.

We picked up speed as we drew closer, and the mob fell back, silent now. They no longer drove us toward our destination but rather followed us to it.

Adelaide led us into the woods. This time, no branches reached out to stop me. No roots surged up to trip me. We broke through the trees to find the coarse sand beach of the Black Lake beneath our feet. The still waters were so dark they mirrored the moonless sky.

And I remembered.

The night on the beach with these girls.

The call of the Black Lake.

The townsfolk lagged behind us, all but a group of thirteen men. One for each girl.

Adelaide's father raised his weapon and pointed it at us. "We cast you out and demand that you go back where you came from, demons."

I studied him and his posse, then looked to the men, women, even children, scattered among the trees, watching and doing nothing. Had the Black Lake whispered in their ears, threading their thoughts with violence, or had evil always lurked deep within them?

This time, no one was going to emerge from the lake during the new moon. Rather, we were being delivered back to it. I felt no fear, only gratitude to the lake for calling us home.

Adelaide was right. We didn't belong in this world, with these people.

I faced the lake and clasped hands with the girl next to me, comforted by her touch. Each girl did the same until we were one long chain. We stepped into the cold water, first to the ankle, then the knee, then the stomach. Numbness encompassed my body and sunk deep into my bones, turning them to ice.

Splashing sounded as the men followed us in. When the water reached my neck, I cast one last glance at the girls. We would be together forever, as it was meant to be.

A hand pressed on the top of my skull and forced my head below the surface, but I didn't struggle or resist. I tightened my hold on the other girl's hand and let the water fill my lungs, breathing it as easily as the mountain air.

The men thrashed behind us as they were sucked below the surface, a fitting sacrifice to the Black Lake.

NIGHT MAERE

MOTHER WARNED ME the Night Maere would come, as she came for all the women in our family. I scoffed, sharing a look with father. We knew these were just more of mother's fantastic ramblings. We did not know she'd die by her own hand within a month's time, clawing herself bloody, and he'd follow shortly after from a broken heart.

Her warning—her prophecy—has come true, though I know not what is real and what is imagined from one moment to the next. Is the demon a symptom of the diseased mind that taints our family, or is an insidious creature who has followed us for generations tormenting us in our sleep?

I climb into bed, my dark mane shielding my face, and my cotton nightgown, my only armor, laced up to the throat. I take a pill from the small bottle on the nightstand. The doctor says I must sleep, that the pills will stop the hallucinations that plague me. I check beneath my pillow for the bundle of lavender and juniper Cousin Hetty promised would encourage sweet dreams, and then switch off the lamp.

Lying back, I pull the heavy comforter to my chin. The room is dark, curtains covering the window, only the barest sliver of light sneaking beneath the bedroom door. The shadows twist and writhe around me in time with my own breathing. My limbs grow heavy, and my eyes shut, though I beg them not to.

I wake beneath the Maere, the comforter pooled at my feet. She sits atop my chest, clawed feet pricking the thin fabric of my nightgown.

My arms, my legs, my head are pinned in place, and each beat of my pulse echoes through my ears. I try to close my eyes, try to escape the visage of the demon above me, but even my eyelids are frozen, immovable. She cannot be real, must be a hallucination.

Her matted hair scrapes my cheeks, steel wool against my tender skin, as she leans forward to peer into my face, her features becoming visible as my eyes adjust to the darkness. A scream swells in my throat, locked within my closed mouth, silently ripping through my brain. The demon wears the face of my mother, smiles wide with lips that once kissed my brow before bed each night.

I can only watch as the Maere's face shifts, bones cracking and skin stretching until I am faced with myself, looking at my own visage as if in a mirror. The demon's claws burrow deeper into my chest, parting skin and muscle, sliding between ribs, piercing my thumping heart. Thick, sticky wetness slicks my nightgown and fills my mouth, tainting my tongue with copper.

The pressure on my muscles eases. I can run now but don't want to, finally understanding. There is nothing above me. My arms fall to my sides, hands slick with blood and fingernails bent and broken, caked with torn flesh. My eyes close and one last, relieved breath slips from my lungs as I complete my metamorphosis, claiming my birthright. I am the Night Maere.

THE DEAD SPOT

SINCE HER EIGHTH birthday, Clare dreamed of screams. The shrieking, laughing, breathless kind that came at the coaster's drop and pulled from her throat as her stomach flipped and twisted.

The very first time she'd exited the Cyclone on wobbly legs, she'd smiled so big her face felt like it might crack right in half. A picture of that first ride, Clare's arms thrown high and her scarlet hair streaming behind her, sat framed in a place of honor next to her spelling bee ribbons, speech and debate society certificates, and soccer trophies.

Every day of her life, Clare's hours were scheduled and charted to allow nothing spontaneous, nothing exciting. Perfectly predictable. Perfectly stifling. Furthermore, she had no say in what was done with her time. Activities were planned and chosen for her based on specific criteria and goals. Even her friends were not her choice. They were the classmates and neighborhood children who had been selected and approved, deemed the right type.

Her mother insisted the opinions of a child were not of importance.

There was one exception to this rule. On Clare's birthday, she was permitted an activity of her choice.

"Don't you want to do something else this year?" her mother would invariably ask, her hair pulled back in a severe bun and her clothes neatly pressed and tucked.

"No, thank you," Clare would answer.

And this year, her sixteenth birthday was no different. She would invite her perfectly acceptable friends to ride the rails of the coaster, to fly with her and be free. Not that they appreciated it, but that was their fault, not Clare's.

You can lead a horse to water, as her mother would say.

Freedom was Clare's obsession. In the dark of her room, out of the grasp of her mother's control, she planned, devising long mental lists of all the things she would one day do. Skydiving, base jumping, race car driving. Nothing was off-limits.

For now, she had one single day per year of freedom. And this year, her sixteenth, *was* different.

Her mother dropped her off at Lakeside Amusement Park, and something amazing happened. Something completely unexpected and unplanned. Clare saw Mia simply standing amid the jostle of the crowd, staring straight up at the Cyclone, her face transfixed as if in worship.

With a confidence Clare had never previously displayed, she walked right up to Mia and introduced herself. They talked easily, laughed as if telling long-held inside jokes, and met one another's eyes with an intensity that made Clare's chest ache.

Mia was like no one Clare had ever met. The human embodiment of a coaster, Mia made Clare feel reckless, free, and a little scared.

Her perfectly acceptable friends were forgotten.

Clare and Mia walked the crowded path through the park, not holding hands, but close enough that their knuckles brushed against one another every few steps.

Darkness had fallen, and the park's rides lit up all around them. Speakers mounted on lampposts blasted pop hits, while the rides themselves played their own lilting soundtracks. Both girls wore shorts and tank tops, the uniform of a warm summer night.

Clare snuck a glance at Mia. Petite and lithe, with striking white-blonde hair worn in a pixie cut that accentuated her almost impossibly pale face, Mia was pretty enough, but that wasn't what fascinated Clare. Mia had a calm confidence, an otherness, a separateness, that made her seem untouchable.

They reached the Cyclone entrance, and Mia stopped and turned, pointed across the park. "The old Speedway is through there."

Clare tore her gaze from the girl and followed the direction of Mia's finger, but she couldn't see anything through the rides, spinning and flashing against the backdrop of surrounding trees.

"It's a big oval track surrounded by sections of bleachers. The kind with a sort of roof on them, to block the sun," Mia said.

Clare couldn't remember the track ever being open, and she'd been coming here for years. "Did you go there when you were little?" But that couldn't be. Clare was sure she'd heard the track had been closed for decades.

"I wish it was still open. Wouldn't you just love to sit in the front row?" Mia ran one hand down her arm, and her eyes took on a dreamy, far-off look. "Feel the wind and heat of the cars as they rush past, spitting little bits of gravel that pepper your bare skin."

Clare swallowed to wet her dry throat. "Why did it close?" she managed.

"There was an accident. A car spun out, crashed into the spectators." Mia grabbed Clare's hand, pulled her up the stairs to the coaster.

"Was anyone hurt?" Clare asked.

Mia didn't answer, must not have heard.

Clare glanced behind her, tried to see the track as they climbed higher, but it was no use.

There was a line for the Cyclone, but Mia tugged Clare past the waiting patrons and went right to the front, where a young guy, probably close to her own age, directed those boarding the ride.

"It's my friend's birthday. So, we're going to cut the line and go first." Mia dropped Clare's hand and stared pointedly at the boy.

"No, it's okay." Red crept up Clare's face, and she focused on the wooden platform. If they got kicked out for breaking the rules, her mother would never let her come back.

"Of course, ladies, come on through," the boy said with a lopsided grin, opening the chain to allow them past.

Clare gaped at Mia. "How did you make him do that?"

Mia shrugged. "He wanted to. I just gave him an excuse."

They slid into the front car, Clare's favorite spot, and pressed the lap bar down tight. Many coaster enthusiasts like the back car, but not Clare. She liked the feeling of nothing but air and wide-open space in front of her.

When the car jumped forward, Clare couldn't suppress her giggle of anticipation.

Mia pressed close, and Clare was acutely aware of every spot where they touched. Her shoulder, her arm, her thigh, and the edge of her hand tingled from the charged contact of Mia's skin.

The *click, click, click* of the car lurching up the track reverberated through Clare's bones. They approached the crest, the starlit night sky blanketing them from above, and the twinkling lights of the park scattered all around them.

The world stopped for a long moment as they hung at the top, waiting, anticipating.

Then they were pitched forward, down, rushing, racing.

Clare screamed, feeling out of control and free and so very happy. She glanced over to see Mia looking straight at her, seeing inside her, through her.

The coaster leveled out, and Clare gulped in a breath.

"Do you hear it?" Mia asked.

"What?"

"Close your eyes."

Clare did. The tug and pull of the Cyclone was even more intense in the total darkness, and she gripped the bar tight.

The ride slowed. Clare's heart thumped in her chest in time with the *click, click, click* of the coaster. Something brushed the shell of Clare's ear, and she gasped at the feel of Mia's lips. "Listen. You can still hear the race cars."

The chatter and laugher and shrieks of the amusement park faded into the background, falling away. The screech of tires and the roar of engines rose above the din. Clare's eyes snapped open.

"I hear them," she said, as they again approached the crest.

Mia pointed—over the park and past the trees. "Do you see?"

Clare squinted, and there it was. Floodlights blazed, illuminating the oval track and sections of bleachers, waiting and ready for the racers and spectators. That couldn't be. The track was abandoned, wasn't it?

They were pitched forward again, and this time Clare didn't scream, could hardly breathe. She felt lightheaded, dizzy, detached. Like she might float free from the constraint of the bar and straight up into the sky.

The car decelerated as they rounded the final slow curve and hit the dead spot, where all the force from the ride dissipated in preparation for the return to the station.

Mia's face was suddenly just an inch away, her breath a soft caress. Clare closed the gap, pressed her lips to Mia's in a rushed kiss that ignited a slow-burning fire in her belly. She pulled back, tasting cotton candy.

They were back at the station, and someone pulled the bar up over their heads. Mia laughed and dragged Clare from the car, down the battered wooden stairs, back out to the midway.

Deliciously numb and warm, Clare let Mia lead her past the attractions, past the food stalls, through the throngs of people and off the paved path. They continued across the grass and into the dimly lit edges of the park, the sound of the crowds growing farther away.

"Where are we going?" Clare asked, her voice husky, almost hoarse.

"You'll see."

Soon they reached the chain link fence that surrounded the park.

Mia dropped Clare's hand to grasp the fence, peeling back a section that had been cut to about halfway up, just enough to allow someone to slip through.

"Can we just go back to the park?" Clare whispered, worry cutting through her contented haze. "My mother—" She bit back the rest of her words, feeling small and much too young.

"I want to check out the old track." Mia's mouth pursed in a pout. "You don't have to come with if you don't want to." And with that, she turned and slipped through the fence and into the tall grass on the other side.

"Wait." Clare rushed forward, wedged herself through the gap. She hissed as a rough edge of the metal link caught on her arm and drew blood. "Mia? Are you there?"

The overgrown weeds swayed in the wind, whispering as they rubbed against one another, somehow drowned out the laughter and celebration of the park behind her.

Clare caught a glimpse of blonde hair ahead, a beacon in the night. She ran through the weeds, uncaring of the dry barbs scratching the bare skin of her legs. The rear of the track loomed closer, the back walls that enclosed each section of bleachers weathered and decaying.

Sweat beaded on Clare's forehead, her neck, her back. The breeze carried a trill of laughter.

"Mia," she said, catching a glimpse of movement in the gap between two sections of bleachers.

Clare found a trail through the overgrown bushes, a path pressed flat by the tromping of feet. She looked back to the safety and security of the park. She could go back, leave Mia behind.

No. Not today. Clare charged forward until she stood between the two sets of bleachers. Just ahead, another chain link fence rose the full height of the bleachers and extended in either direction, probably put in place to stop those in the stands from running onto the Speedway. There were no floodlights, just the illumination of the surrounding city lights. The track itself was cracked and overgrown with weeds. Several rusted cars still sat on the asphalt. Sadness clutched Clare's stomach as she walked along the fence, trailing her fingers along the barrier. She stopped short when she reached a section of the fence that had been torn and crushed inward toward the bleachers.

"I knew you'd come," Mia said from just behind Clare.

Clare jumped and pressed a hand to her chest. "I thought I'd lost you."

"Come on." Mia climbed the first few rows of bleachers to get around the fallen fence, then descended toward the gap that led to the track.

Clare scrambled after her, followed her out onto the cracked, weed-ridden asphalt, Mia's mere presence causing her breath to catch.

"I just love being under the lights, feeling their glow. Don't you?" Mia raised her face, eyes closed.

The lights flooded to life, and Clare gasped. She squinted up at the orbs lining the oval track, felt like she was staring into the sun.

Mia placed her hand on Clare's shoulder. "It's such a perfect night for the stock car races. We were lucky to even get tickets, with this crowd."

The din of distant city traffic faded under the roar of the race crowd. Clare spun around, taking in the now repaired bleachers packed with hundreds of people. Their whoops and cheers filled the air. Clare's appetite perked at the smell of hot dogs and popcorn.

"I've never been to a race before," she said, beaming at Mia. Her mother would never have approved this, even on her birthday.

Mia grabbed Clare's hand and tugged her toward a car just a few feet away, a shiny silver coupe with the number sixteen painted on the hood and side doors. Clare stopped short, looking around with a frown. "We should stay in the stands, shouldn't we?"

"We're competing in the race, silly." Mia opened the passenger-side door and urged Clare inside.

Clare settled into the leather seat. The smell of dust and mold tickled her nose as the lights dimmed and the crowds quieted. Confusion clouded her mind. Why was she here?

Mia plopped down in the driver's seat, and the flowery smell of her perfume, or maybe it was just the smell of her, cleared the fog from Clare's head. They were actually going to race, and maybe even win! Clare would place the trophy on her shelf, and it would be taller and shinier than any of the others.

A gleaming skull key chain dangled from the ignition, and when Mia turned it, the engine growled to life, sending purring shudders through the metal frame of the car. When Mia stepped on the gas and revved the engine, Clare couldn't hold in her laughter. The raw power of the car filled her body with buzzing excitement. And to have Mia next to her, sharing this with her, was a feeling like none she'd ever experienced.

Mia threw the car into drive, and they shot forward on the track, squealing around the first curve. Clare was thrown back against the seat, pinned by the inertia of the car, just like a coaster. The windows were open, and Clare thought for a moment that this was strange, but the thought fled as fast as it had arrived. The hot summer air tugged at Clare's curls, and the scent of burnt rubber singed her nose.

Several sets of brake lights snaked in front of them, and blinding headlights pressed in on them from behind. The car lurched forward as Mia gave it more gas.

"Faster! More!" Clare cried in delight and braced herself against the dash, her heart hammering in her chest. Next year, she'd ask—*insist*—on the Speedway for her birthday.

Cries from the spectators filled the air, rising in the night, and Clare couldn't stop smiling. They screeched around another corner, and Clare felt herself being flung into the air. Her stomach flipped and twisted as she flew, her body light as air, able to float right up into the stars. A laughing scream tore from her throat at the visceral freedom of the flight, at the feeling of being truly alive.

Clare didn't feel the sharp jab of the torn chain link fence or the rough edges of the bleacher steps as she landed in the stands, her arms and legs splayed out in impossible angles. Her hair fanned out around her head in a macabre scarlet halo, and though blood trickled from the corner of her mouth, a smile still split her face.

Mia crouched down beside Clare, brushed a stray curl from her forehead with a gentle touch. "I knew you'd stay."

There were no more bright lights, no more cheering crowds, no more racing cars. No more smell of popcorn or burnt rubber. There was only darkness and rot, rusted metal skeletons on the track, and the lingering sound of Clare's screams carried by the wind.

BURNT EMBERS AND BLUEBIRDS

"If the doors of perception were cleansed everything would appear to man as it is, Infinite. For man has closed himself up, till he sees all things thro' narrow chinks of his cavern."

—*William Blake*

THE PAPER-DOLL GIRLS enter the library like a whisper, feet silent on the linoleum floor. People move instinctively out of the way as if nudged by an invisible cloche that protects the pristine girls from contamination.

Sitting in the back corner of the library, at a wood cubicle that allows me to hide should they look my way—something they've never done—I watch the two of them walk down an aisle, running their hands along the spines of the books, their eyes closed. They seem to choose based on feel.

One stops, says, "Here," and extracts a book from the shelf. Dropping to the floor, they sit cross-legged in the aisle, knee to knee.

They wear Mary Janes and prim dresses fit for girls younger than they, made from fabric of flowers and butterflies, belted at the waist with red ribbons that match the bows in their hair. They look just like the paper dolls from Grandma's old newspapers, back issues of *The Boston Herald*. She'd pull a paper from the pile, flip the yellowing pages until she found one of dolls, and sit me on the floor with a pair of scissors. The dolls are gone now, burned up in the fire, heavenly company for Mom and Grandma, I hope.

The paper-doll girl who chose the book holds it close to her face, examining the title, rubbing the cover against each cheek, inhaling the musty sweet scent of the pages, before opening it on her lap. Though she leans down, her hair doesn't move, staying perfectly in place in a graceful drape over her shoulders and back. She reads a page with eyes and fingers, then passes the book to the other girl, where the process is repeated, back and forth with each page-flip. I picture square tabs sticking from their shoulders, their hips, their heads.

A patron walks down the aisle, asks them to move, but they continue with their circuit, as if hearing nothing. Some days there are raised voices or complaints to the librarians, but the paper-doll girls are a part of this place, offered the same deference as priests in a church.

When the announcement comes, stating "The library will close in ten minutes," they stand in unison and place the book back on the shelf. The girls walk to the end of the aisle, sucking their paper-cut fingers, and stop to stare at me. I freeze, forget to hide under the weight of their unnatural eyes, twin pairs of iridescent opals. They each lift a hand and wave. At me.

Before I can wave back, they leave through the stairwell door. Once inside, they climb the stairs from the basement library with the graceful steps of ballerinas, round the landing between flights, and are gone. Until the next day. I know this because one night after the library had closed, I followed them to see where they go.

As soon as the stairwell door closes, I rush from my cubicle to their aisle—in the 700 section today—and locate the book. Third shelf from the top, five sections in, black jacketed spine with bold white lettering. *William Blake, Complete Collection.* I rub my cheeks on the cover, which features a man kneeling within a flaming disc. I inhale the scent of the pages and rub my finger along the closed edges. Pain slices through my tender fingertip, and I smile, collecting another hint of their blood to mingle with my own.

Clutching the book to my chest, I pass the rows of tables and the groupings of comfy chairs, step up to the counter, and push the book across the counter to the librarian, along with my library card.

"How are you today, Farrah?" she asks. She's the nice one who gives me food sometimes.

Hair hiding my face in a very un-paper-doll-like way, I focus on my grimy tennis shoes and say, "Fine."

The machine beeps as she scans my card and the book, then she slides both back to me. A white bread sandwich in a baggie sits atop the stack. My stomach growls.

"Thank you," I say, tucking the card in my pocket before taking the book and my dinner.

"See you tomorrow, hon."

I rush from the counter, past the last few people heading up to check out their books. Once in the stairwell, I unwrap the sandwich and eat it in a few big bites. Creamy butter and jam, strawberry with chunks of fruit and tiny seeds that stick in my teeth for later. Since running away from the foster home, I mostly survive on dumpster scraps, and I've learned to eat quickly or be chased off.

Folding the baggie, I slip it in my pocket. They work well to keep my feet dry when the rain is too heavy. The backpack containing my worldly possessions is wedged beneath the stairs, and I pull it free. My breath locks in my lungs at the sight of red ribbon tied to the handle in a perfect bow.

I PLACE *WILLIAM* *Blake, Complete Works* on the returns cart at the end of the librarian's desk and slip past the other patrons. Morning is the busiest time, the worst time, but the dozen or so people littering the entry area don't bother me today. I slip past them, through them, my mind clear and full-to-the-brim all at once. Sitting in my normal spot at the farthest cluster of cubicles, I adjust the ribbon in my hair, uncaring that the bow is out of place with my grubby sweatshirt and jeans.

The paper-doll girls have never shown me anything so incredible as Blake's paintings. Art is a favorite of theirs, along with fashion, astrophysics, Buddhism, parapsychology, magic, and dead languages. Sometimes they read fiction, too. Everything from children's books, like *The Very Hungry Caterpillar*, to literature, like *The Bell Jar*. That one made me sad, reminded me of Mom.

But Blake affected me more than any book yet. I knew him as a poet, but his paintings unlocked something inside me his words never had. Sitting in my makeshift tent tucked at the back of the alley behind the bus depot, I pored over his images of God and angels, of spirits and fantastical worlds. Tears streamed from my eyes, cleansing the dirt and grime from my face, carrying away the loneliness and pain I'd been holding onto so tight. Releasing me.

The stairwell door slams, and the paper-doll girls arrow toward the aisle closest to me and stop at my cubicle.

"Hi," I say, my voice an awkward squeak of nervousness.

One holds a book, not chosen from a shelf but brought from wherever they go when the library closes. They angle their heads down the aisle, as if inviting me to follow them, then disappear between the shelves. I rush after, stumbling, my toe catching the leg of a chair.

The paper-doll girls sit cross-legged at the end of the aisle, not facing each other, but forming two sides of a triangle. I slow, unsure of myself, embarrassed. The one holding the book places it in the empty spot and points at me. My mud-slicked shoes squeak on the floor, and I cringe. Panic rises in my throat, because I think they'll laugh and tell me I don't belong, because this will be taken from me like everything else, and I'll be alone like always.

The bow in my hair tightens, a pleasant pressure, a reassurance, and I take the last few steps. With trembling hands, I stoop to pick up the book and sit down, pressing my knees to theirs. They look at me with eyes made of fractured moonlight, then cast their gazes down to the book in my lap. Covered in rough, woven fabric printed with hieroglyphics and mathematical equations, it has no title. When I open the cover, a soft breeze smelling faintly of freshly turned earth tickles my nose.

Each page holds only one word, a girl's name written in a blotchy brown paint. Savannah. Pria. Becky. Hiro. Inez. Poppy. And on and on. I read each one, trace the shape with my eyes, let the taste of each letter bloom on my tongue.

Until I reach a blank page near the back. And I know. "For me?" A flutter fills my stomach, my throat, my head.

The paper-doll girls beam at me, revealing dimpled cheeks. "You belong with us," they say, though their mouths don't move.

Warmth envelopes me as I caress the page, *my* page, running my fingers over the gilded edges until they slice into my fingertip.

Not blotchy brown paint at all.

I scrawl "Farrah" in looping script, blood flowing as if dipped from an inkwell. Raising my finger, I blow on the page, watch as red turns to brown.

A tingling starts in my hands, runs up my arms, my legs, my scalp. My vision blurs slightly, then sharpens, and I see everything around me more clearly than ever before, see the molecules that vibrate within the books on the shelves, the floor, even the air itself. The paper-doll girls glow with an internal light that hums within their chests, each heart a prism barely encased in muscle and bone.

My own chest cools, extinguishing the last of the burnt embers that coat my heart. A dress appears atop my clothes, white cotton printed with bluebirds. My throat tight with gratitude, I try to speak, but no words can describe this feeling, this elation, this freedom from loneliness. I'm one of them now, one of so many sisters. "Thank you," I say.

One of the girls reaches out and takes the book from me, her smile widening, her teeth sharpening. The other girl smiles to match, and their eyes shift, turning from opal to obsidian.

I gasp and skitter backward.

The girls stand, and in a flash of orange, their paper-doll disguises are burned away to reveal what's underneath. Clawed hands and feet, snouts like jackals, twisting horns in place of perfect bows.

They're not the angels from Blake's paintings at all, they're the demons.

I try to run, but they lash out with spiked tails, wrapping my arms and holding me in place. Heat flashes over my exposed skin, singes each tiny hair, and I whimper. It's just like that night, with Mom and the matches.

Fleshy wings sprout from their backs and wrap around me, cocoon me. I scream until my voice is hoarse, until the fire eats my tongue and melts my throat. No one comes, no one cares. Maybe they only see paper dolls.

"You belong with us," they growl. "You're welcome."

Flames devour every patch of skin, every muscle, every bone, every thought. All those names, all those poor girls. I hope they're at least waiting for me.

MR. CHEW

MR. CHEW ISN'T real.

He's a monster from an old nursery rhyme, a myth passed from the big kids to the little ones.

Mr. Chew, all dressed in black,

His jaw unhinges with a crack.

An older girl at the playground scared me with the rhyme so bad I'd cried when I was younger. The other kids laughed. My brother, Jason, is eight now, so I passed the rhyme down to him, like any good big sister would. Maybe I wanted to give him a scare, too.

But I'm the one who's scared.

Mr. Chew wears a too-small black suit, with cuffs stopping mid-forearm, leaving his spindly hands dangling. Liver spots dot every patch of pale, exposed skin on his oversized bald head, long neck, and bare feet. But it's his eyes that betray he's a monster—bulbous, white orbs, with blood-red irises pitted by black pupils, and no eyelids that I can see. He doesn't blink, only stares.

Watches you with blood-filled eyes,

Grabs with fingers sharp as knives.

I sang Jason the rhyme a week ago, and I've seen Mr. Chew every day since. He comes closer each time. At first, he was just a hulking figure standing at the end of the block. Today, he's posted on the sidewalk in front of our house. I walk past him to wait for the bus and feel a rush of hot air, smell a hint of rotting fruit.

"You're not real," I say, still watching him.

"Who?" asks the skinny, shaggy-haired boy just ahead of me on the sidewalk, waiting with the others for the middle school bus. He's a year younger than me and new, or else he wouldn't be talking to me.

"Him." I point at Mr. Chew.

"There's no one there." The boy cocks his head to the side.

Heat climbs up my neck. "I know."

Late at night, the man will creep,
Eats the bad ones while they sleep.

"Crazy Cammie." Drew, the coolest of the cool girls, sing-songs my nickname and bumps me from behind, earning giggles from her friends. She eyes my threadbare gray T-shirt and stained, ill-fitting jeans. "Crazy *Crusty* Cammie." She pushes me, knocking me into the boy.

"Watch it," he says, grasping my arm.

At the press of his fingers on my skin, my pulse swells to fill my ears like a crashing wave, and I shove him to the ground.

His face reddens, and he scrambles back to his feet. He won't look at me.

I should apologize, but my teeth are clenched too tight, my throat closed off against an anger I can't let escape.

Drew snickers, and my fists itch to find her face, but I jam my hands in my pockets instead. Remember what the counselor said. I control my temper. It doesn't control me.

The bus pulls up, and I'm the first to climb the steps, slumping into a seat at the very back. As we pull away from the curb, I watch Mr. Chew.

There is no chance to run away.

Mr. Chew will make you pay.

His eyes swivel in their sockets, and the black pupils settle on me, bore into me.

See you soon, his eyes seem to say.

I GET OFF the bus after school and stand frozen on the sidewalk.

Mr. Chew has moved again.

He waits on the front porch, his bare toes poking over the edge. My heart thumps hard enough to crack my chest wide, but I force myself to walk up the stairs. I'll get the belt if I try to climb in through a window. I ease past him, closer to him than I've ever been. The black pupils at the center of the red irises aren't pupils at all, but holes which want to suck you in. His sweet stench wafts by, and those black pits follow me. He doesn't move, doesn't even seem to breathe.

The worn porch boards creak, alerting Mama Theresa to my presence, and the door swings open. I rush inside and close the door behind me, though I know very well doors can't keep monsters out.

A lipstick-stained cigarette clasped between her lips, she dumps baby Trev into my arms.

His full diaper smooshes against me, sending a whiff of crap to sting my nose.

"He needs changing," I say.

She removes the cigarette from her mouth and swipes it past my bare arm, laughing when I flinch.

I should know better than to think she'd burn me where someone might see.

She heads back toward the living room, her ass swishing back and forth beneath purple velvet sweats.

Trev gives a whiny cry, and I smooth back his fine hair. "Shh, shh. It's okay."

He's only been here a month, hasn't learned yet not to cry.

I prop the baby on one hip and enter the kitchen. The linoleum floor is almost as cracked as the front walk, a definite tripping hazard. And still, the foster-care people think this is a good place for kids.

Jason stands on a wooden milk crate at the sink, doing dishes. He's just tall enough, even with the boost. I haven't gotten used to this yet, seeing him every day. After our parents died in the accident, he was taken in by a real nice foster family. He almost made it out. But they sent him back. Four years, he was with them, and they returned him.

He won't tell me why.

I place a peck on his cheek.

"Ewww." Having recently learned about girl cooties, he rubs at his face with one hand, leaving a trail of soap suds.

I lean back against the counter. "How was school?"

"Stupid," he says, avoiding my gaze.

"Did something happen? You can tell me. Maybe I can help."

"I can take care of myself." He scrubs at the frying pan with a Brillo pad, and I notice the scrapes marring his knuckles.

He's turning out just like me. "Fighting isn't the answer. You know that."

"Whatever."

I sigh. "I'll dry after I get Trev cleaned up." I bump Jason's shoulder with my arm, my chest tight with the knowledge I'm the reason he's here. Sitting next to me in the backseat, he just wouldn't stop bawling. So, I had grabbed his arm and twisted, like the kids at school did to me—a snakebite, they called it. Dad only looked away from the road for a few seconds. By the time Mom screamed, it was too late.

Maybe that's why Mr. Chew is coming for me.

I make my way down the hall and into the room the three of us kids share, furnished with a mattress and playpen. Trev wiggles in my arms and his face scrunches, a sure sign he's about to let loose.

"Shh, shh." I close the door to drown out his cries so Mama doesn't hear.

After grabbing a towel from the laundry basket, I place it on the mattress and plop Trev down.

I tug down his shorts, and the sight of the sickly yellow and purple bruises marring his chubby little thighs turns my stomach. I try to take the brunt of Mama's anger, but it's not enough. She hurts the boys, and I can't stop her.

Maybe dying won't be so bad. A little pain, and then nothing but relief.

MR. CHEW CAN'T be real, but he's here, standing at the foot of the bed. Jason snores beside me, his tattered blanket wrapped around him, and Trev is passed out in his playpen.

A tremor starts in my bones, works its way outward until I'm shaking so hard I might shatter. I want to burrow under my own blanket, but there's nowhere to hide, nowhere to run from the things I've done to deserve this.

At least I can protect the boys from *him*.

I force myself to creep across the room and step into the hallway. The house is dark, except for the sliver of light from the television spilling out in strobe-like flashes from beneath Mama's bedroom door. The voices from one of her idiot reality shows screech through the wall.

Mr. Chew follows and walks a slow circle around me. The smell of him clings to me—decay with a hint of syrupy sweetness.

My legs are too wobbly, too weak, to try and run.

"It was just a snakebite. No one was supposed to die," I say before fear steals my voice. I should beg to be spared, say I'm only a kid. I'm trying to be better. But maybe I'm really bad deep down inside, and maybe a little piece of me wants to die.

He stops and faces me, gnashing his teeth.

His jaw snaps open with a crack, and I flinch. Too many teeth, too sharp to be human, line the gaping hole which has become the lower half of his face.

I press my hand to my mouth and swallow back a scream. No, no, no. I don't want to die. Not like this.

"Mr. Chew," Jason says.

I gasp and look over my shoulder to see him peeking from our bedroom doorway. "Go back to bed. Now. And close the door."

"It's okay, Cammie. I called him."

"What are you talking about?" I ask in a harsh whisper.

Mr. Chew inclines his head toward Jason, then turns to Mama Theresa's door, reaching one clawed hand out to grip the doorknob.

Jason creeps up next to me and takes my hand. He's riveted, eyes gleaming with excitement. "He's going to help us hurt them all."

Rasping breaths seize my lungs. I watch Mr. Chew twist the knob, and Mama T's door swings open with a creak. Flickering light bathes Mr. Chew, bleaching his already pale skin, and he steps into the room. Jason tugs me forward until we can see inside, where Mama T lies naked, sprawled atop her blankets, with an empty bottle of whiskey beside her. Drunken snores saw from her throat.

Mr. Chew slams the door, cutting off our view, and I sob in relief. I have to drag Jason away, back to our room, but even there, even with the blaring of her television, I can't block out Mama's screams.

MR. CHEW IS real. Jason called, and he came.

Mama Theresa lies splayed across her bed, her mouth a grimace of pain, even in death. Her body is covered with bites, jagged wounds where the man chewed off softball-sized chunks of her flesh. Blood covers almost every inch of her skin, soaks the sheets, and drips onto the floor in great, red, shining pools. There must be buckets of it. The room stinks like the worst of Trev's diapers mixed with copper and sweat.

Bile surges up my throat, and I turn away to puke on the floor.

She hurt me, hurt the boys, but she didn't deserve that. No one deserves that.

I stumble down the hall and into the bedroom to scoop Trev from his playpen. "We'll go to the neighbors', call the police. Say we found her like that." I swallow hard, taste the vomit coating my tongue. "It's going to be okay. We're going to be okay."

Jason sits on the edge of his mattress, tying his sneakers. "Don't worry. No one can hurt us anymore. Or else Mr. Chew will get them."

"You can't call him again, Jason. Not ever."

Jason grabs his backpack from the floor and slings it over his shoulder, like it's morning and he's off to school. "Mama Theresa tried to tell me what to do, too."

My knees buckle, but I catch myself with my free hand, bracing it against the door frame.

Jason runs down the hall, his shoes squelching on the vomit-soaked shag carpet.

I stagger after him with Trev cradled in my arms. My vision jumps and blurs, but I manage to make it through the house and outside. I suck in a deep breath, but that horrid smell of pain and death sticks inside my nose.

Jason skips along the sidewalk, singing.

"Mr. Chew, all dressed in black,
His jaw unhinges with a crack.
Watches you with blood-filled eyes,
Grabs with fingers sharp as knives."

The glow of the full moon does nothing to wipe away the image of that room, of what Mr. Chew—what *Jason*—did to Mama. I shuffle along, the concrete scraping my bare feet.

Jason continues, his voice cutting through the quiet calm of the night.

"Late at night, the man will creep,
Eats the bad ones while they sleep.
Sing this song, again and again.
Say his name, invite him in."

Jason stops at the neighbors' walk and looks back at me. "Hurry up, Cammie. We need help." His lip quivers, and he sniffles. "Someone hurt Mama Theresa. Please, help us. There's so much blood."

His face changes, shifts as the monster he's become resurfaces, and he actually *giggles*.

Directly ahead of Jason, on the sidewalk, Mr. Chew appears, the pale skin of his face and hands smeared red.

I lurch to a stop, clutching Trev to my chest. Spiders of panic crawl up my spine and across my scalp. "Go away. Leave us alone!"

The man is inches away from Jason, but my brother doesn't react, doesn't even seem to see the man.

"Who're you talking to, Crazy Cammie?" Jason turns down the neighbor's walk, humming that horrible rhyme.

Mr. Chew looks at me and raises his long, clawed, index finger to his mouth.

Shh.

Gnashing his teeth, he watches Jason race up the steps of the front porch. Watches his next victim.

The final verse of the song lilts through my mind.

Careful, careful, what you dare.

Not all survive his bloody stare.

Tears blur my eyes, scorch my cheeks. "You can't be real. You're not real!"

Trev starts to wail, and I fall to my knees on the sidewalk.

"I just wanted to scare him a little," I say, my voice choked by sobs. Mom. Dad. Now Jason.

And it's all my fault.

Mr. Chew drifts after my baby brother, leaving a trail of rotting fruit wafting in the night air.

CRIMSON CLOVER

MAMA LAY ON the kitchen table, screaming until her voice was no more than a bullfrog's croak, the midwife's soft words no comfort. After a full rise-and-fall of the blistering sun, my baby sister, Clover, came. When she opened her mouth and cried, the clouds gathered and released a torrent of rain on the parched land. Mama died smiling, with a crimson Clover in her arms.

I would've liked to see Clover smile, too, but Daddy said God sent her for a bigger purpose, one that required suffering. Each day we'd poke her or pull her hair to make her cry, and the rain would come. Crops grew, and we all had enough to eat and drink, even the dogs and horses. But it took more and more to make Clover cry, punches and kicks and long pins. The townsfolk each took a turn, each did their part.

Then Clover couldn't stop crying, even whimpered in her sleep like a starving kitten searching for her mama's teat. The rain poured down until it flooded the fields and choked the roads and uprooted houses. Daddy took her out back and buried her, made sure to fill her little mouth with dirt.

The rain stopped, but I still heard Clover crying. We all did. Daddy tried stabbing those same pins in his ears, and it stopped every other sound but her. I buried him, too, to stop him screaming. Now I wait for blessed starvation, Clover's cries my only company.

UNRESTFUL DOGS

BARKING DOGS WRENCHED Mave from the deep, dark well of sleep. She struggled to escape the bonds of the heavy damask comforter, and sat up straight, her heart fluttering in her chest like a bird trapped in a too-small cage, unable to stretch its wings. The yips and howls faded, never truly raising an alarm, and she chided herself for her silliness. Dogs were made to bark at many things—a passing fox, a scampering bunny, a strong gust of wind, or crack of thunder. There was no monster here. Not tonight.

She eased to the edge of the bed, her high-necked cotton nightgown clinging to her clammy skin, and stepped into her plush slippers. Swaying on her feet, she reached out to steady herself on the carved bedpost, feeling the ornately rendered vines twist and curl beneath her fingers. A scream sounded, high and sharp, and she slapped her hands over her ears to stop the phantom sound that liked to follow from her nightmares.

No daylight streamed through the window, so she knew she had once again slept through the rise and fall of the sun. She was just so terribly tired. Perhaps it was the constant, gnawing fear, slowly eating away her energy and occupying her waking thoughts until sleep was the only respite. Or would be, if not for the nightmares. She wished she was brave, like her older sister, Berna. But no, Mave had always been the delicate one, the helpless one, the burden. Not that Patrick had ever said such a thing to her. He loved her, flaws and all.

She perched on the small, cushioned bench in front of the dressing table, carved to match the bed, and squinted at the reflection she cast in the gilt-framed mirror. Relief settled her pulse at the sight of her own pale face, more plain than pretty, blurred and insubstantial, sunken in the cheeks and around the eyes, but hers. This daily act, this forcing herself to look upon her own reflection, was the most courage she could muster. Some days, the nightmares followed her from sleep, peering from her eyes through lizard-like slits, gnashing their pointed teeth in her mouth, licking her cracked and bleeding lips with a forked tongue.

Dream demons, Patrick called them. Just remnants of sleep. And on the bad days, he would hold her face in his hands and describe what he saw. Just Mave, just a woman so lovely he would gladly drink in the sight for all his days. Her own vision was tarnished and failing, clouded with dark shadows, but her beloved would be her eyes, her truth.

Footsteps sounded somewhere in the house, a rhythmic sound treading across old wood. Acting of their own accord, her ears strained to place the direction and proximity of the sound, though she scolded them for doing so. Patrick had risked so much to protect her, to hide her away. To nose in his affairs would be very unbecoming, if not outright ungrateful.

Mave picked up her mother's pearl-handled brush and pulled it through her auburn hair, her thoughts still on the footsteps. There were other noises, too. Creaks and thumps that gave her the feeling of a house filled with people. Like the orphanage at night, quiet but full and restless. Sometimes she imagined she heard those same soft whimpers from her childhood.

The footsteps were probably just servants. Patrick had to have a staff, being a man of stature and with a home of this size. A frown tugged at Mave's lips as she tried to picture the outside of the house, the layout of the estate, the surrounding countryside. No image came forth.

Her memory seemed to be deserting her, betraying her, just as Berna had. As much as Mave concentrated, she couldn't recall how she'd gotten here, to this room, or how long it had been. And what was it her sister had done to betray her? She placed the brush back in the dressing table drawer, eyes catching on the clear glass jar tucked within.

Barely larger than her pinky, it was topped with a black, rubber cork. She'd found it beneath the bed, tucked against one leg. Something stopped her from telling Patrick of her find, maybe the thought that he would call it nothing, say she was silly for hiding the insignificant thing away.

She picked up the tiny jar, examined the trace of liquid inside, watched it coat the glass. To her, the jar seemed not insignificant at all, some deep instinct inside her insisting that it was quite significant. Important. She tucked her find back in the drawer, out of sight, not wanting to think any more about the thing tonight.

Mave went to the window, wishing she could open it and breathe deep of fresh air flavored with the crisp lavender that blanketed the hillside. But the sash had been fastened in place, dear Patrick having nailed it himself to keep her tantalizing scent contained. Red still stained the wood from when she'd clawed at the sill and torn off her fingernails in an attempt raise the window. She'd been in such a state that day, so consumed by the demons, she'd tested even Patrick's infinite patience.

A door slammed, and she startled, turning her back to the wall and clutching at the lace adorning her throat. Her mouth went dry as her mind conjured visions of Patrick being taken away. Visions of the soldiers, masked and armed, beating him, stabbing him, throwing him in some deep, dark dungeon.

Mave had been designated as an offering to the monster, after all, but her beloved had intervened. If they ever found out where she was, what he had done—

Metal scraped against metal as a key turned in the door's lock, and Mave scampered across the room to wait. The door opened, and there was her Patrick. A smile lit up her face as he held a finger to her lips in a reminder to keep quiet. He slipped inside the room, carrying a tray covered with a silver dome, and closed the door behind him.

Clasping her hands at her waist, she waited as he set down the tray on the bedside table. Only after he opened his arms did she rush into her beloved's embrace, pressing her face to his and inhaling the intoxicating pine scent of him.

"My love," Patrick murmured, smoothing a hand over her hair. "Did you miss me?"

"I always miss you." She pulled back to gaze at him, a vision of golden skin and dark hair. Her beloved's face was the one thing she could see clearly, now and in her memories. She again tried to recall this house, any part of it besides her room, but couldn't.

Her distress showed on her face before she could stop it, and he asked, "Is it the dream demons again, my darling?"

"No, no. It's a good day, today." Mave hesitated, not wanting to admit her deterioration. "My memory, it's so fuzzy. Tell me, how long has it been? That I've been here?"

"Not long enough for the monster to forget, my love, but soon. I promise."

She frowned, her thoughts knotted and tangled. "There was something else. About my sister, I think—"

"She doesn't deserve your attention."

"You say she left me…" She trailed off, unable to recall that horrible day.

"She left you for the monster, like a coward."

"But she was always the brave one." Yes, that was right. She remembered Berna protecting her as a child, making sure she was fed and clothed after their parents had passed, saving up enough to get them both free from the orphanage. Those had been hard but happy times.

Patrick stood and his mouth took on that twist Mave disliked very much, the one that said she had displeased her beloved.

"Am I not brave? Did I not risk everything to take you in, to protect you?" he asked.

Mave's eyes burned with the regret of her words. "Of course, my darling, I'm sorry. You are my everything."

He sighed, tension still gripping his shoulders.

"Will you lie with me tonight, my darling?" she asked, wanting to burn away her hasty words under the heat of passion.

"We'll see. I have the dogs to tend to. They're restless."

"Do you fear the monster is close? That tonight the beast might find me?" Her voice shrank to that of a frightened child.

Patrick took sympathy on her, forgiving her insult, and stepped close to grip her hands. "You are well-hidden, my love. I won't let the beast take you."

Mave blew out a breath and straightened her spine, trying very hard to be brave for her beloved.

"Eat, now. You need your strength." He took the lid off the tray to reveal mashed potatoes and chunks of meat in a brown sauce.

She reached out for the plate, when the barking of the dogs sliced through the night in warning.

He went to the door, his eyes darting toward the curtained window, perhaps wondering what awaited him in the darkness. "I'll be back when I can. Stay quiet, my love."

"I will. Please be careful, my darling," Mave said, and her beloved was gone.

A tiny part of her wanted to fling open the door before the lock clicked in place, to run far away, to go somewhere that didn't have any monsters at all, if there was such a place. But she had to trust Patrick to hide her, to keep her safe. Pulse hammering in her throat, she picked up the spoon and shoveled several chunks of meat into her mouth. The sooner she finished eating, the sooner she could crawl back beneath the heavy covers of her bed. She hoped there would be no quiet sobs tonight, no phantom scream, that her mind would give her a few moments of peace.

THE METAL DINING trolley, three levels high and stacked with four domed serving platters on each level, sat waiting for Patrick in the hallway. He uncovered the next plate and pulled a small glass vial from his shirt pocket. Perfected over the years through his veterinary practice, the mixture of sedative and hallucinogen worked well to keep his precious ones from endangering themselves, kept them mostly convinced that he was their savior.

While he'd invented the monster who demanded sacrifice, there were countless real evils that would devour his lovely Mave and all the others, given the chance. He simply couldn't allow them to endanger themselves. They must be protected from the world, preserved.

He waited for a moment outside her door, the corner of his mouth ticking up at the sound of the spoon scraping the plate. Mave was one of his favorites. She had become such an obedient pet, not like her sister.

CLUTCHING AIR

ALMA HAD NEVER been particularly brave, but fear could drive people to do things they didn't know they were capable of, and since the night of the break-in, there was nothing that scared her more than being alone in their apartment. Her mom, who worked nights, now always left the television on in an attempt to simulate company, but the canned laughter and commercials wiggled their way into Alma's mind and gave her bad dreams.

She started by raising the paint-chipped window sash and staring down at the metal fire escape that descended from their third-story apartment, wondering how many bones she would break if she tumbled over the wobbly railing. The next night, she actually stepped onto the rusted metal of the mesh platform for a full minute, feeling terrifyingly free as the wind whipped down the alley and through her cropped curls. On the third night, she climbed down the rickety stairs, gripping the inadequate railing tight while focusing only on the next step down. She reached the hanging ladder and descended until her sneakered feet rested on the last rung, the last chance to turn back, but she'd come too far. She let herself drop the last six feet, landing silently in the darkened alley below. Shadowed humps of piled garbage bags lined the wall beside her, and a rat skittered past. She held perfectly still, swallowing her scream. Invisibility was the best protection from many of life's dangers, a hard lesson she learned too late that now informed her every move.

Though her mom had tasked her older brother Tony with looking after her, he was sixteen and didn't take it seriously. He'd intended to sneak out unnoticed, as he had been doing most nights for the past year, and as he had done that night the bad man broke in. Her mom said they shouldn't tell him about what happened to Alma, that he'd feel guilty for something that wasn't his fault, not really. So, she kept the secret and hated him a little more every day for not knowing.

Alma decided she was done being left alone, and she wanted to know where her brother went at night to "do his art," as he called it. She identified his hangouts in daylight by finding his tag, most often placed in the alleys between the row of five run-down, twelve-story, brick apartment buildings that made up their neighborhood in Green Hill.

That night she didn't have to search long, finding him just one building over from their own. She crept down the shadowed alley and hid behind the first of several dumpsters, listening to the sound of Tony and his friends spray painting the wall. The smell of rotting garbage filled the air, and she swallowed down a gag, closing her eyes to focus on the rattle of the marbles inside the paint cans, the white noise of the spray.

When a police siren whooped and light splashed the entrance to the alley, she froze. Metal clanked against concrete as someone dropped a spray can, her brother and his friends running away from the mouth of the alley to escape over a chain link fence. To her relief, the cops moved on without investigating. She did not want to talk to the police ever again, knew they weren't interested in protecting her, not really.

Peaking around the dumpster, she looked both ways to make sure she was alone. A lock of her hair escaped from beneath her beanie, and she tucked it back in, setting a mental reminder to cut her curls short again. She'd gotten in the habit of downplaying her girlish appearance, including dressing in Tony's oversized hand-me-downs.

The discarded spray can rolled across the pavement and stopped at her feet. She picked it up and shook it experimentally, the hair on her arms rising at the reverberating clack of the marble against the sides of the can. Walking over to the brick wall, she surveyed the tags her brother and his friends had left. Most were simple, like Tony's signature "ANT," a play on his full name, Anthony. She'd seen other, more developed graffiti in her explorations, but these weren't yet up to that level.

Trembling a little, she raised the can to a blank section of wall and pressed the nozzle, dispensing a dense circle of yellow paint that dripped trails down the brown brick facade. A harsh, chemical smell clouded the air, somehow cleansing and antiseptic. She inhaled a full, deep breath for the first time in months, feeling the invisible particles coat the inside of her nose and creep into her mind. Reaching out, she touched the dribble, felt the pleasing sting of it on the bare skin of her finger.

The spot was nothing artistic— just a bright, clumsy dot—but it didn't matter. She'd left a mark that people would pass by and see, wondering who did that and when.

ALMA STOPPED FOLLOWING Tony, instead sneaking out in search of her own spaces to practice and perfect her art. During the day, between classes and often during them, she drew in her sketch book. After a month, she had a tag worthy of Green Hill, a place that sung of secrets and struggles: "LALA."

It didn't take long for her talent to surpass Tony and his friends, who spent half their nights drinking, meeting up with girls, and generally causing trouble. Her bold purple LALA tag captured the attention of people in the neighborhood, who talked about the new, mysterious street artist, wondering who "he" was. She even overheard Tony trash-talking her, saying how much better he was than this newcomer.

Alma never said anything, didn't want anyone to know, and she had gotten good at keeping secrets. She even wore rubber gloves to prevent paint stains on her hands, though she liked the look of it on her skin, the feel of the abrasive chemical brand. Imagining herself as a young Banksy, she fantasized about crossing paths with her idol some late night in a dark alley, exchanging the knowing look of ghosts.

Tony stopped tagging shortly after she started. For him it was a phase, an experiment on a path to other forms of vandalism and self-expression. But after being deflated, hardly able to take in enough air to continue breathing, tagging filled Alma up with pure oxygen. Fear still pressed at the edges of her mind, but for the first time since the break-in, it didn't crush her. The bad man thought no one was home, and she'd discovered him rifling through her mother's room. Instead of robbing them of replaceable possessions, he'd robbed Alma of something irreplaceable. Her nighttime excursions, her new secret, made the weight of the old one easier to carry.

While she still drew and advanced her artistic talent, she also spent time location-spotting and planning. She learned more about Green Hill than she ever knew, got to know Harry, who ran the bodega, Kendhra, who delivered the mail, and Lupe, who owned the hot dog cart and comped Alma more often than not. She became intimately familiar with the neighborhood's alleys and rooftops and abandoned storefronts. While she saw poverty and pain, she also saw beauty in camaraderie and community.

Those experiencing homelessness, who camped on the sidewalk, and who Alma once thought to be scary, soon grew names and stories, became people she worried about when the temperatures chilled. She carried a thermos of hot coffee, paper cups, and packs of peanut butter crackers to share with those who were often hungry or thirsty or cold. She became a recognizable face, the quiet but friendly girl from building 781. But by night, she was still LALA, and thought of herself as a ninja, stealthy and unseen, riding the shadows of the buildings and creating art for the people of her neighborhood.

By fifteen, she perfected her unique wildstyle and, needing a new challenge, moved on to heaven-spotting—placing tags in hard-to-reach and dangerous places. She exercised quietly in her room, building her strength and agility, and conducted research. Using the laptop issued to her through school by a grant to fund the education of impoverished kids, she sought out YouTube videos and learned how to construct homemade harnesses, how to make gaff spikes that attached to her boots, how to use carabiners and belays. After selecting an out-of-reach spot, she gained access through fire escapes or roof hatches or power poles. Dressed in black and visible only by her headlamp, she hung over the edges of buildings, or dangled from bridge struts to place her art.

She knew every inch of her neighborhood, which made it hard to ignore the creeping wave of development that ate at the edges of Green Hill. One by one, homes and businesses and apartments were remodeled or torn down to the foundation, and she felt the world around her warping into something new and grotesquely clean.

Her art became a weapon. While her wildstyle pieces were hard to read, as they were meant to be, they were an undeniable brand on the neighborhood. She knew better than to out herself as LALA, but she enrolled in every available art class offered at school and began to share another version of herself during the daylight hours.

When the apartment building next door to her own was sold to a developer for a modern office complex, she joined the protesters in front of the building and attended community meetings to give voice to the people like her being pushed from their own community by rising rents. While she felt good about that work, she became increasingly hoarse as her protests fell on ears deafened by the promise of money.

Those experiencing homelessness that had become her friends were arrested for loitering or illegal camping and taken to jail, their mere presence a crime. There was no one left to drink her coffee and eat her crackers. Paint quickly covered the buildings and bridges, obliterating the street art created not just by Alma, but by so many who called Green Hill home. She ran into more and more taggers at night and stopped caring if they recognized her face. Alma and LALA became one, the quiet girl from the neighborhood and the passionate street artist. She cried happy tears when she overheard Tony bragging to his friends that LALA was his kid sister.

All the street artists worked together to combat the spreading gentrification, but they couldn't keep up. The developers started by blacking out any graffiti, then paid artists from outside the neighborhood to apply murals depicting parodies of diversity that took up entire walls and extended along sanitized alleys strung with fairy lights.

When a Starbucks opened in the closed location of Harry's bodega, Alma got ahold of an extension ladder and covered the side of the building with wildstyle street art depicting the names of all the business owners who had been pushed out or driven under. Walking by the next morning, she saw a worker hosing down the wall and watched her message stream from the surface and disappear into the gutter. The building had been sprayed in anti-graffiti paint, a silicone coating that protected the pristine brick surface.

Next, she turned to stencils and altered posters, using the facades of the corporate chains that displaced decades-old mom-and-pop shops as billboards for her commentary on the changing landscape of Green Hill. When she plastered the windows of that same Starbucks with flyers of the company's own logo, altered to include devil horns, fangs, and a portion of their mission state-ment "One Neighborhood at a Time," it took the owner a full week to scrape the storefront clean. It seemed like a victory, a pushback against corporate infestation, until the police installed security cameras on every lamppost in the newly developed areas, more concerned about those properties than they'd ever been about the true victims of crime.

While local stores closed, forcing the owners and their families out, and those suffering from homelessness were arrested, others seemed to just disappear. The faces of her friends appeared on flyers, begging for anyone with information to please call, while the police insisted these poor kids were just runaways.

Alma began to feel like an outcast in her own neighbor-hood, more and more of the people she passed on the street looking decidedly unlike her. These new residents glared at her and her neighbors, mouths twisted and noses crinkled in disgust. Just days after her art was scraped clean from the Starbucks windows, her mother broke the news they were being pushed out, would be forced to move because their building had been sold to developers for conversion to high-end condominiums. They couldn't afford to stay.

Alma refused to stop fighting, more resolved than ever to reclaim the neighborhood, to show the encroachers who truly belonged in Green Hill.

ARMED WITH A backpack full of stencils and spray cans, she descended the metal stairs with a stealth that came from practice. She'd procured a signal jammer to block the feed on the newly placed cameras, and she and her tagger friends, the ones still left, intended to plaster the shiny new stores with paint and posters every night until they drove out the corporate devils.

Hood drawn over her head and hands in the pockets of her sweatshirt, she made her way along the street, shoving past couples and groups enjoying a late night out. Sidewalks that had previously been bathed in shadow were now lit by an array of expensive bars and restaurants that none of the original residents of the neighborhood could afford. Though they'd agreed on a midnight meet up, she saw not a single other street artist among the interlopers.

A glass-fronted gallery had popped up where the local food bank used to be, and she stopped to peer through the windows. Her backpack slipped from her shoulder, the metal cans clanking against one another as she stared inside at the exhibit titled "Banksy Unauthorized." Elegant patrons holding flutes of champagne prowled the space, assessing works she'd only glimpsed in Reddit threads and grainy YouTube videos. Works that now hung on pristine white walls and were adorned with price tags. A banner of street-art-style ads plastered to the window in a neat row proclaimed the pieces had been reclaimed from their homes, torn from the streets and alleys where they'd been placed by the artist. All had been authenticated as the work of Banksy, and though the artist himself hadn't approved their sale, they were available for the right price.

Bile filled Alma's mouth, and she spat on the glass. Body shaking with anger, she turned down the alley that ran between the gallery and bar next door, unzipping her pack as she went. The alley was under construction and not yet lit, so she was able to hide in the comfort of the shadows. An open bag and several spray cans lay on the concrete, making her think her friends had been there, but she didn't see any evidence of their art.

Her outrage wouldn't wait for company, so, working quickly, she sprayed LALA in the largest bubble letters she could manage without ladders or other equipment, using shades of purple, with accents of blue and yellow to bring the letters forward from the surface. Green Hill was her neighborhood, her *home*.

Panting, she stepped back to survey her work. Starting at the top corner, the letters appeared to fade and sink into the surface of the wall itself.

"What the fuck?" she whispered. Was this some new type of anti-graffiti paint?

In the span of just a few minutes, her design had disappeared entirely.

She retrieved a can of bright red from her bag and went back to work, reapplying the letters and accenting them with white and pink. The same thing happened again.

The paint sank beneath the surface of the brick until the wall appeared pristine and unmarked.

"Fuck you!" she screamed. These assholes thought they could stop her, but they couldn't. She would not be silenced.

She grabbed her yellow paint and tagged the wall in a rush of wildstyle letters, chaotic and powerful. But just like the rest, the message disappeared as soon as she'd finished her work.

The spray can slipped from her hand, joining the other cans discarded on the ground, and Alma backed toward the mouth of the alley, shaking. How could this be happening? How could this be possible?

She ended up standing in a pool of light beneath the newly installed halogen streetlamps, near a crowd that was lining the sidewalk to get into a hip new bar. A man in a suit and woman in a sequined dress walked toward her, but didn't spare her a glance, didn't even acknowledge her presence. Anger vibrating in her bones, she tried to shove past the couple, but only stumbled and fell right through them. On her knees now, she lashed out with a fist and watched as it passed through the man's expensive, leather boots. She grabbed at the woman's wrist but grasped nothing.

Cowering back against the wall where her homeless friends had once huddled and slept, Alma held her hand up in front of her face. Her flesh had turned transparent and pale, like frosted glass. Chest tightening, she looked up and down the street, hoping to spot someone from the neighborhood, sure that they would be able to see her, be able to help her.

The street she had known, had grown up with, was gone, replaced by a suburban paradise of chain stores, posh housing developments, and pristine office spaces. And the only people left were the new ones, the predators who had taken over, who had consumed or chased away everyone Alma cared about.

"Help," she managed to call out as she climbed to her feet. "Can someone please help me?"

The people in line showed no reaction to her plea.

"Something's wrong!" she yelled, trying to grip the arm of the woman closest to her but only clutching air.

No matter how loud she shouted or how many people she tried to grab, no one saw or heard her. Panic wrapped her chest, and she ran into the street to wave down a car. It drove right through her, leaving behind thick exhaust that clogged her spectral throat and stung her eyes.

Chest hitching with sobs, she retreated to the alley, to the place she found her voice again after it had been stolen the first time. Her pack and discarded spray can still lay on the concrete, but when she tried to pick up the yellow paint, she couldn't.

"No!" she cried, trying again and again to pick it up but failing. She stared at the other discarded cans and wondered about her friends, about what had happened to them.

Body wilting from exhaustion and fear, she slumped back against the pristine wall, where she'd once sprayed a brilliant, yellow circle. But the building, the wall, the neighborhood, had no room for her or those like her anymore. Alma sunk into the surface as if drowning in thick, viscous liquid, her hands flailing uselessly about until she was swallowed entirely. Her vision went black, her eyes open but seeing nothing. She screamed until her throat burned, but her voice was absorbed into the wall around her, even her own ears deaf to the sound, to any sound at all.

The spotlight of a police car swept across the alley, one of the last undeveloped and unlit spaces in Green Hill, but the only evidence of Alma was her abandoned backpack and spray can. She would never be seen again, except on the missing-persons posters fixed to the light posts daily by Tony and her mother. Alma and the others who'd disappeared cried out for help from their smiling photos for a few short moments each day before the flyers were promptly removed by a community service officer or conscientious resident aware of the law against posting handbills. The newly redeveloped neighborhood had to be kept in pristine condition, and everyone knew the kids in the photos were just runaways.

EDGE OF DECAY

THE MUSIC WAS and is my only relief. In the past, a small, used Casio keyboard squeezed a little of the rot from inside me every time its off-key notes squeezed beneath my bedroom door. Even my parents, whose anger at each other, at the world, at what their lives had become, stopped shouting when hearing the sound of that little keyboard. Now, a single organ plays a very different song—a thumping, repetitive bassline, overlaid by a careless smattering of high notes in a minor key that twists something inside me, at once both heart-wrenching and comforting.

Death changes a person's song.

I was thirteen when we moved into the trailer covered in corrugated steel, painted a yellow that was already sun-faded and chipping. The backyard butted up to a gravel road that, once crossed, led to open fields filled with prairie dog burrows. Past the fields, a set of train tracks ran. Prairie dog yelps and the blare of the horn often woke me back then, but the dogs and the trains are long gone.

That first day, I raced Sam for the bigger room at the front of the trailer. At five years old, his size alone meant he couldn't win, a fact I used to my advantage, as big sisters often do. I won the race. Wood paneling covered every inch of every wall in our new home, lending a darkness to the space that no amount of lamp light could dispel. But daylight helped, and my room had two windows: a large bay that took up the entire wall facing the street, and a small side window. The organ window.

Our parents' room sat at the opposite end of the trailer, far enough away that some of their fights were muffled. Sam's room was right beside mine. When he played the Casio keyboard he'd spent a quarter on at a rummage sale, the notes drifted down the short hallway, seeped beneath my door, and reminded me there was one good, pure thing in my life.

Other sounds fought hard to stop me believing in that good thing. The train rushing past on rusted tracks, metal scraping on metal in a sound that hurt my bones. My parents' fights, yelling that turned to the thump of fists on flesh. The prairie dogs screaming when a hawk invaded their happy little dens to snatch one of their babies with a sharp beak.

When Dad drank too much, he and his friends made a game of hurling potatoes against the living room wall. The hollow thunk shook the walls and settled in the pit of my stomach. To someone else, their chuckles might have sounded like they were having fun, but it had a pained quality to it, like a child's laughter hiding tears after a cruel snake bite twists skin and muscle.

One bad winter, fierce hailstorms raged, a pounding of ice on metal that threatened to tear our trailer apart. Afterward, I dreamt of machine gun bullets firing through the bay window in a deafening roar, their path unleashing an explosion of glass and dust and tattered curtains in the air.

After the nightmares and the potatoes and the screams, the Casio brought me back, drew my head just enough above the water that I could suck in a deep breath before being pulled back under. Until the day there was no more music.

That night I lay in my bed, which sits flush against the small, side window, with the headboard against the wall below the bay. My good thing was gone, and I waited, almost hoped, to drown. The breath of the first note of the organ filled my lungs, and I sat up, knowing there was nothing in my room capable of making that sound. It continued to play, coming from right beside me. I looked out the small window by my bed, but saw only an open patch of grass, the neighbor's driveway, and his trailer. At the time, a man lived there with his dog, a German Shepard kept outside all winter, with only a rickety doghouse to shelter it from the brutal cold. The dog would whine, soft and sad, until I had to clamp my hands over my ears.

The phantom organ played all night, the notes blooming from the air itself. I didn't ask my parents if they heard it, knew they hadn't. The song was just for me, and it's been visiting me, playing for me, every day since. I'm coming closer to understanding what Sam is trying to tell me.

Shoving the snarls of my dark hair from my face, I wrap an old Afghan tight around my shoulders and push back the curtain to climb onto the ledge of the bay. Two pieces of corrugated metal form a wedge beneath the window, the enclosure for the trailer's hitch. I'd used it to sneak out a few times, as a step between the window and the ground, but the edges of the metal are sharp and sliced deep into the meat of my palm once. Maybe it got a taste for blood that day.

A blanket of white covers the streets and dead patches of grass and caving roofs, the unmarred brightness of it hurting my eyes. There are no neighbors left, only abandoned trailers sporting smashed windows and sagging frames, sandwiched between empty lots marked by driveways of cracked cement. My hometown has curled in on itself, contracting in a last effort to stay alive. It has already sacrificed the dying appendages on the outer edges of town, left them to rot and decay.

As if summoned by my sadness, the music joins me and I smile, glad for the company. Slipping from the ledge, I sway in the middle of my room. The notes are always soft, even from my spot in bed, but they live inside me now. My mind replicates the song and amplifies it, until my bones vibrate with music.

The tune is different today, as if some vital harmony has been added, and Sam's song is finally complete.

My stockinged feet soundless on the carpet, I drift through roomy bedroom door and into the hallway that takes me past his room. It's empty now. Not a single toy, piece of furniture, or shred of clothing remains. They were all burned in a giant heap in the backyard, even that little Casio. The jagged ring of burnt earth is still there beneath a thin layer of snow.

The wood grain of the walls shifts and curls, warping into the innocent, giggling figures of children. His ghostly playmates, I hope, so I don't have to imagine he's alone in the dark. Let's play, the children call, scampering from one snarl of woodgrain to the next in writhing twists. They lead me through the living room, past the recliner and sagging sofa where my parents sit staring blankly at the TV, their sun-weathered faces drooping like melted wax. They still hate each other, hate everything, but after Sam, they went quiet.

The children frolic along the walls and into the kitchen. In a whirl that surrounds me, they turn to shadows that slide across the Formica table and skitter across the ceiling. The figures solidify again on the far side of the kitchen, resuming their wood-grain dance on the wall and cabinets above the stove.

"Make yourself useful and cook dinner." My dad sneers from his spot in the recliner.

I smile. That's just what Sam wants, too. I fill a pot with water and set it to boil over the licking, blue flames of the gas burner, then pull a box of mac and cheese from the cupboard. He loved hot dogs in his, cut into little discs. We don't have any hot dogs, but there's another special ingredient that will make dinner perfect.

The music whispers.

The pot bubbles, and I stir in the macaroni, watching the half-moons swirl in the water, in a dance of their own. I join in and turn circles on the cracked linoleum. Mom says something insulting, but I'm insulated in my cocoon of music, so the words just bounce off me without even leaving a mark.

I strain the noodles and stir in the powdery cheese, extra margarine, milk, and the special ingredient. The Day-Glo orange is muted a bit by the brown powder, but no one will be able to tell in the dim light. After dishing my parents' dinner into two bowls, the music pauses, opens a space for a memory.

Dad had taken Sam up onto the roof. I tried to stop him, but we had leaks, and "the boy needed to learn hard work." He was only eight, too small to labor under the hot sun, too inexperienced to apply hot-tar sealant. When footsteps sounded overhead, small ones running, heavier ones stomping, I knew Dad had lost his temper. A roar rose in Dad's throat, and I followed the footsteps through the living room, down the narrow hallway and into my bedroom, throwing open the curtains on my bay window.

Sam fell. Or maybe he was pushed. Either way, he tumbled off the roof and slammed down onto that wedge of corrugated steel. He saw me, his wide, brown eyes meeting mine, and his mouth formed the shape of my name. His body bent unnaturally over the metal, his head and legs dangling over either side. A scream tore from my throat as I threw open the window and reached for him, grabbed one small, limp hand. But his eyes had already gone dull. Blood trickled from the corner of his mouth and oozed from his torso, dripped down the rippled metal like a grotesque waterfall.

Sucking in a breath, I blink away the image of that terrible day. Tears burn my eyes, and I grip the edge of the counter. I know his death wasn't my fault, but I could have stopped what came after. Mom and Dad didn't scream or cry. They didn't try to save him or call an ambulance. While I huddled in the window, sobbing, they cleaned up "the mess." There were still a few others living in the park then, so they had to be quick. They wrapped Sam's tiny, broken body in an oil-stained canvas tarp and shoved him beneath the porch, then bleached away the blood. After dark, they removed the skirt of metal just below my side window, dug a hole, and buried my baby brother in an unmarked grave. Mom and Dad made sure to tell me I'd join him if I ever said anything to anyone.

I waited in my bed for the darkness to consume me, but Sam saved me, helped me find life again in the sorrowful melody of that organ. We both waited for something to happen, for someone to realize a little boy was missing, but no one ever came. This town and all the people in it were too busy trying not to die themselves. Sam knew what had to be done, and he told me through that wrenching melody. *We're done waiting.*

My special ingredient, powdered Rozol, sits on the counter. The stuff is old, bought way back when we first moved in to keep the prairie dogs from infesting our yard. Mom and Dad probably forgot we still have it, tucked safely beneath the sink, behind the rat traps. After one use, they stopped using the poison, the effects too cruel even for them. The prairie dogs didn't scream after ingesting the Rozol, just moaned and cried while blood seeped from their eyes and mouths, the poison eating them away from the inside.

"Dinner's ready," I say, picking up the bowls and delivering them to Mom and Dad. They shovel the mac and cheese into their mouths as they continue to stare at the TV.

Sam's music swells beside me, a pillar of sound taking physical form, and I know he's with me. The wood grain writhes around us as the children gather to wait, to watch. The organ plays, the bassline thumping like Dad's heavy footsteps on the roof. But Mom and Dad can't hear it, don't know that death is coming for them. I smile, anticipation raising the fine hairs on my skin when Mom coughs, spraying the air with a mist of blood. A spattering of high notes peppers my ears. A giggle.

ACKNOWLEDGMENTS

THIS COLLECTION INCLUDES one of the first short stories I ever wrote and one I wrote just for this collection. *The Dead Spot* captures my journey as a writer and my obsession with sad and lost girls. As a woman in the world, I can't help but tell these stories. While there aren't a lot of happy endings here, I hope I've captured the strength and fire inherent in girls everywhere.

Thank you to my partner, Zach. I'm so lucky to be on this journey with you and thank the universe every day to have you as my best friend. Thank you to my editor, Rob Carroll, for helping me make my work the best it can be and for giving me a home at Dark Matter INK. Thank you to Sara, Christi, Caleb, and Carina, who took the time to read and blurb this collection. I respect each of you so much and am truly humbled by your words. Your generosity and willingness to lift up others in the horror community is a gift and an inspiration.

Thank you to J. A. W. McCarthy, whose writing never fails to cut me to the core, and who contributed the introduction to this collection. To see such kind words written by someone I respect so deeply is an incredible honor. I seriously teared up when reading the introduction for the first time. To Alexis, Saytchyn, Tracy, and Brian, who have critiqued various stories in this collection and helped make them the best they can be. To my many writer friends and mentors, you are a gift that I am so grateful for. To my family, my biggest cheerleaders, I am so lucky to have you all in my life.

Thank you to all the publications who have accepted my work and allowed me the opportunity to share my stories with the world. Nine of the stories in this collection are reprints, and I am so appreciative of the editors that first gave them a home.

Lastly, thank you to my readers for taking this journey with me. It is truly one of the most humbling experiences of my life to know that there are those who read my words and are affected by them.

—Angela Sylvaine

ABOUT THE AUTHOR

ANGELA SYLVAINE IS a self-proclaimed cheerful goth who writes horror fiction and poetry. Her debut novel, *Frost Bite*, and debut short story collection, *The Dead Spot: Stories of Lost Girls* are out now. Angela's mall slasher novella, *Chopping Spree,* will be available fall of 2024. Her short fiction and poetry have appeared in over fifty anthologies, magazines, and podcasts, including *Southwest Review, Apex,* and *The NoSleep Podcast.* She lives in the shadow of the Rocky Mountains with her sweetheart and three creepy cats. You can find her online at angelasylvaine.com.

CONTENT WARNINGS

"Astronaut Dreams": *Violence, Death of a child, Suicide*

"The Bride": *Violence, Death*

"New Hue": *Violence, Death of a child, Classism*

"Playing Tricks": *Mental illness*

"Sorry, We're Open": *Violence, Death, Suicidal thoughts*

"Antifreeze and Sweet Peas": *Violence, Death, Suicide*

"If Heard, Please Call": *Violence, Death of a child*

"Starved": *Violence, Death, Cannibalism, Mental illness*

"Return of The Wilderness Girls": *Violence, Death of a child, Cannibalism*

"Night Maere": *Violence, Mental illness*

"The Dead Spot": *Violence, Death of a child*

"Burnt Embers and Bluebirds": *Violence, Death of a parent, Death of a child*

"Mr. Chew": *Violence, Child abuse, Bullying, Death of a parent*

"Crimson Clover": *Death in childbirth, Death of a parent, Death of a child, Child abuse*

"Unrestful Dogs": *Abduction, Abuse*

"Clutching Air": *Implication of sexual assault, Death of a child*

"Edge of Decay": *Violence, Death of a child*

A NOTE ABOUT REPRINTS

Please note the following stories are reprints:

"The Bride," *Supernatural Horror* from Flametree Press June 2017

"Playing Tricks," *It Was All a Dream* from Hungry Shadow Press October 2022

"Antifreeze and Sweet Peas," *Not All Monsters* from Rooster Republic October 2020

"Starved," *Consumed* from Denver Horror Collective December 2020

"Return of The Wilderness Girls" based on "The Blacklake Girls," *Disturbed Digest* June 2017

"The Dead Spot," *Terror at 5280* from Denver Horror Collective November 2019

"Mr. Chew," *The Dread Machine* November 2020 and *It Calls from the Veil* July 2022

"Crimson Clover," *Apex Magazine* Patreon May 2022

"Edge of Decay," *Dark Recesses* April 2022

Frost Bite by Angela Sylvaine
ISBN 978-1-958598-03-0

Free Burn by Drew Huff
ISBN 978-1-958598-26-9

The House at the End of Lacelean Street
by Catherine McCarthy
ISBN 978-1-958598-23-8

When the Gods Are Away by Robert E. Harpold
ISBN 978-1-958598-47-4

Grim Root by Bonnie Jo Stufflebeam
ISBN 978-1-958598-36-8

Voracious by Belicia Rhea
ISBN 978-1-958598-25-2

The Bleed by Stephen S. Schreffler
ISBN 978-1-958598-11-5

Chopping Spree by Angela Sylvaine
ISBN 978-1-958598-31-3

Saturday Fright at the Movies: 13 Tales from the Multiplex
by Amanda Cecelia Lang
ISBN 978-1-958598-75-7

The Off-Season: An Anthology of Coastal New Weird
Edited by Marissa van Uden
ISBN 978-1-958598-24-5

The Threshing Floor by Steph Nelson
ISBN 978-1-958598-49-8

Club Contango by Eliane Boey
ISBN 978-1-958598-57-3

The Divine Flesh by Drew Huff
ISBN 978-1-958598-59-7

Psychopomp by Maria Dong
ISBN 978-1-958598-52-8

Disgraced Return of the Kap's Needle
by Renan Bernardo
ISBN 978-1-958598-74-0

Haunted Reels 2: More Stories from the Minds of Professional Filmmakers Curated by David Lawson
ISBN 978-1-958598-53-5

Dark Circuitry by Kirk Bueckert
ISBN 978-1-958598-48-1

Soul Couriers by Caleb Stephens
ISBN 978-1-958598-76-4

Abducted by Patrick Barb
ISBN 978-1-958598-37-5

Cyanide Constellations and Other Stories
by Sara Tantlinger
ISBN 978-1-958598-81-8

Little Red Flags: Stories of Cults, Cons, and Control
Edited by Noelle W. Ihli & Steph Nelson
ISBN 978-1-958598-54-2

Frost Bite 2 by Angela Sylvaine
ISBN 978-1-958598-55-9

The Starship, from a Distance by Robert E. Harpold
ISBN 978-1-958598-82-5

Dark Matter Presents: Fear City
ISBN 978-1-958598-90-0

Part of the Dark Hart Collection

Rootwork by Tracy Cross
ISBN 978-1-958598-01-6

Mosaic by Catherine McCarthy
ISBN 978-1-958598-06-1

Apparitions by Adam Pottle
ISBN 978-1-958598-18-4

I Can See Your Lies by Izzy Lee
ISBN 978-1-958598-28-3

A Gathering of Weapons by Tracy Cross
ISBN 978-1-958598-38-2